Enigma Sun

- A Novel -

Marilynn J. Harris

Cottage Publishing

Cottage Publishing
Boise, Idaho
www.marilynnjharris.com

First published by Cottage Publishing 5/22/2015

ISBN-13: 978-0692456729 (Cottage Publishing)

ISBN-10: 0692456724

Printed in the United States of America

For information or to order more books please visit our website:
www.marilynnjharris.com

Or Contact:
Cottage Publishing
8530 W Targee Street
Boise, ID 83709

Dedicated to my dear friends
Dr. Keyes and his beautiful wife Patty

TABLE OF CONTENTS

One

Back Home

Several weeks had passed since our horrifying adventure with the giant bees and the brutal winds in Tower County, and in some ways it felt like a lifetime ago. The entire incident now seems unbelievable and unreal. It is as if everything that happened to us took place in another time.

The killer bees, the devastation, all of the mutilated animals and the deaths and destruction were beyond our comprehension. The entire episode is so mind-boggling that my husband and I never even told anyone about it or even tried to discuss the situation with anyone else.

We knew the truth about the bees and violent winds, but no one seemed to really care about the truth, they just wanted to get everything cleaned up and back to normal.

The entire state of Idaho had silently moved on as if nothing abnormal had taken place in that community. The television and newspapers had tactfully swept the disaster under the rug and they had gone on to other things as if the situation in Tower County had never even happened.

The clean up project had been stamped confidential and none of the turbine specialists or bee keepers was allowed to discuss the project with anyone. The entire situation seemed really strange, but because no one ever talked about what had caused the problems there in the first place, we too kept quiet about what we had witnessed.

Darrell and I never planned to get so involved in the frightful problems taking place over there. We just intended to find our friends and bring them back to Boise where they would be safe from the havoc of the tornado-like winds, but once we got there, one thing led to another and we ended up right in the middle of a terrorizing nightmare.

Suzanne and Gene had been close friends of ours for over thirty years, ever since our children were small. They had lived here in Boise most of their lives, but they decided to move to Tower County a few years ago to be closer to their family. We talk to them on the phone at least once a week, but we rarely got to see them as often as we would like to.

When the channel 7 news reported about the turbulent winds that were taking over Tower County, we couldn't help but be concerned. Each time we would talk to our friends on the phone they sounded more and more upset. Suzanne was horrified because the winds got stronger every day. She told us that the violent winds never stopped, only at night.

You could hear the fearfulness in her voice with every phone call. The unexplainable winds blew so intense that it broke out several windows in their house and destroyed the roof and continued uprooting many of the old giant trees that surrounded their property. The menacing winds were so loud that I could hear the violent howling through the phone lines each time we talked on the phone.

I begged our friends to come back to Boise, and they were considering it the last time that I talked to her. Then all of the phone connections went down. When the phones in their area stopped working and I could no longer reach them to find out how they were doing, I became even more concerned.

The nightly news reported many strange happenings in their community. It told of several missing people and hundreds of dead cows that the local farmers had discovered scattered throughout the fields out by the giant wind turbines.

We feared for our friends' lives. After the phone towers stopped working we decided to get in the car and go over and rescue them. They only lived about four hours away. We knew that if we left early in the morning we could be there by afternoon and just pack up our friends and bring them safely back to our house until the terrible winds had ended.

But everything changed once we drove over there; things were not that simple. The conditions were much worse that we could have ever imagined, the closer we got to their community the more vile the situation appeared. The circumstances were far more desperate than we could have ever guessed they would be.

A policeman stopped us at a checkpoint on the outskirts of the city and we were told to turn around and return to Boise because they were not allowing anyone into the destroyed area because it was not safe. The officer at the checkpoint told us that most of the town had been evacuated and no one was allowed to travel into the cluttered streets alone. He said that a large portion of the town was in total ruin.

I pleaded with the officer to let us go in and find our friends. I told him that we couldn't just give up and go back home once we were there and could see the devastated area for ourselves.

As we stared off into the direction of their community we could see the despicable turbulence and smog rising from the valley. The image was horrifying. The entire area looked like a war-zone from another country. We could not take our eyes off of the disaster. It was the most daunting sight we had ever witnessed in our lives.

My husband and I knew that we could not just turn around and leave our good friends in this horrendous situation. They would never turn their backs on us. It was not right to just drive away and abandon our dear friends in their time of need. We had to find them and take them safely back to Boise.

After talking with the policeman for a short while he finally told us "If you really want to sit here and wait for several hours until after dark when the military trucks arrive, you can drive in with them." He told us, "Most of the area has been evacuated and the authorities do not want anyone going in alone and running the risk of getting lost or injured."

I cheerfully thanked the nice officer and we parked in the designated section and promised to wait until nightfall when we could drive in under the protection of the Army.

Later on that day as we sat waiting for the military vehicles to come I spotted a strange dark cloud over near the wind turbines as I watched the surrounding area through the binoculars. I didn't realize it at the time, but it was that mysterious dark cloud that would eventually tie us together with the happenings in Tower County.

Hours later when the massive military trucks arrived we were allowed to follow the convoy down into the shattered community. The entire area was destroyed and the eerie atmosphere was beyond explanation. The ruined community was unrecognizable; it looked like something out of a low-grade horror movie. Who would ever believe that strong winds could cause so much destruction?

When we finally reached their damaged house we discovered that they had already been rescued, and by then we knew that it was too late for us to leave and head back to Boise. We were already trapped in the horrifying calamity that was taking place in their community.

We had promised the military commander that we would stay with the Army convoy. They didn't want anyone separated from the rest of the group and driving around the hazardous area alone. With all of the heavy damage to the town most of the roads were destroyed and the two of us were afraid to try to travel out alone anyway. It would be too difficult to find our way around by ourselves, so we stayed with the military vehicles as we had been instructed to do. That is how we innocently ended up in the middle of the nightmare in Tower County.

If I close my eyes I can still hear the sickening howls of the violent winds and I can vividly picture the flying road signs and garbage that were scattered throughout the area. The air was so polluted and bizarre that I was sure the town would never be livable again.

I don't know if I will ever be able to totally forget that dreadful night when we followed the huge Army vehicles in through town. In some respects we were grateful to be allowed to go in with the soldiers to check out the properties and to try to find our friends. However, what we saw as we drove into town that night was only the beginning of a nightmare that we feared we may never live through.

As I sat there in my front room reminiscing of that horrible time, I realized that I had been daydreaming so much that my coffee was getting cold. It wasn't until I brought my coffee cup up to my lips that I noticed how violently my hands were shaking. Just thinking about our frightening struggles made me even more thankful that we were safely home in Boise. We needed to just move on and forget the terrible ordeal caused by the mysterious winds.

Yesterday, I read a small article that was written about the bees that had been found in Tower County. The article appeared very insignificant and it was on the back of the newspaper located in the far left corner at the bottom of the page. The article said that after the violent winds had stopped, the authorities discovered large masses of giant dead bees scattered throughout the meadow on the outskirts of town.

It appears that most of the towns-people could not accept the fact that their town had actually been destroyed by giant honeybees; so the bees were rarely spoken of. Rumors around Idaho had rapidly spread that it was the malfunctioning of the wind turbines that had caused all of the devastation, and the destructive bees were almost completely forgotten. Everything had been taken care of out at the wind turbines, so the town knew that something like this could never happen again and it was time for everyone to move on.

My husband Darrell and I would remain among the select few who actually knew and accepted the truth of the killer bees that had taken over the wind turbines. We were two of the only people who had actually seen the giant bees and witnessed the horrifying winds.

Darrell and I had seen the gigantic bees several different times; the first time was after they had discovered the body of the entomologist from Washington in the small laboratory after he had been killed by the bees.

Dr. Keyes, the lead meteorologist from Pennsylvania had shown us a glass container with several neatly arranged dead bees that they had collected from the lab after it had been cleaned out. Our small group had the opportunity to hold the case of bees in our hands for several minutes and carefully study the huge insects.

I remember how magnificence the giant honeybees looked as they lifelessly appeared through the impeccable glass cage. The enormous bees were amazing. It was easy to see why the entomologist was so enthralled with the beauty and uniqueness of the crossbred creatures.

They were so much larger than a honeybee that you would normally see on a small farm or in someone's backyard. They were marvelous giants. Studying the large honeybees was like stepping back in time to the days of the dinosaurs. They were unlike anything any of us had ever seen before.

We would have never been shown the huge bees if we had not been in a private meeting with Dr. Keyes right after the entomologist had been killed. We just happened to be meeting with him and his team about something else when a lab person brought in a glass container with the bees carefully arranged inside a case display. Each of us was in awe of the magnificent crossbred giants. They were absolutely beautiful.

The second time that we saw one of the giant honeybees was at a restaurant in Mountain Home, Idaho when we were on our way home from the Tower County safety location. We had just had dinner at a restaurant and we were heading for our car when we heard people shouting and laughing over near the restaurant window. A man had discovered one of the large bees out in front of the building. The bee was dead and the man was so proud of what he had found that he was holding it in his hand and shouting for everyone to come and see it.

Within a few seconds there were people gathered around the man commenting about the strange creature. People were hollering and squealing because the bee was so huge. When my husband and I walked over to see what everyone was screaming about; I instantly panicked because I couldn't believe that one of the bees was in Mountain Home, only 39 miles from Boise. How did it get there? My husband and I cautiously walked all around the area where the man had discovered the dead bee, but we found nothing. There were no other bees in the area, so we got in our car and drove home.

We had seen the bees two different times, so no matter what the television or newspaper told everyone we knew the bees were real, and we knew why the wind turbines malfunctioned.

Soon their community would be totally restored and the giant bees would forever be just an unexplainable legend. It no longer mattered to us; our friends were safe, the winds were gone and we were just thankful to be home and to have that horrendous nightmare behind us.

Suzanne and Gene seem so much better. They are constantly in our thoughts and prayers, and we are encouraged every time we talk with them on the phone because they sound happier and more content every day.

They are so impressed by the way their community worked together to put the entire town back in order. They told us how all of the fallen trees and cluttered debris that we had driven through only a short time ago had been cleaned up and hauled away. A massive dump-site out at the edge of town would soon be the only evidence of a once destroyed community. The broken windows and roofs had been replaced in the houses and the businesses and most of the families have safely returned to their homes.

The roads have been patched and crews have been working around the clock to remove the garbage and trash that had once covered the entire vicinity. It is amazing to hear how swiftly the horrendous disaster has been cleaned up and restored. They told us that even the burned out section of town had been leveled and would one day be rebuilt.

My husband Darrell and I were there during the brutal winds, we were trapped right in the center of one of the raging cyclones. We knew first hand how terrifying the outburst could be. We personally witnessed the total destruction that the sadistic winds had created, but it was time for us to forget the winds and get on with our own lives.

TWO

Time to Ride

It was summertime and we were thankful for the beautiful warm sunny weather and we planned to enjoy every minute of the nice weather conditions. After being trapped inside of a giant cavern for several days without seeing daylight we developed a whole new respect for freedom and sunshine.

It was nice to be riding motorcycles with our Tuesday night CMA dinner group again. I know that someone in our motorcycle group recalls the day of the darkness just as I do, because they sent me the cute THINKING OF YOU card with the picture taken a year ago as we traveled on our tedious journey in search of the light. But I still do not know who sent it to me.

I keep the photograph hidden away in my dresser drawer, and I take it out and look at it every day or so. I cherish the wonderful picture of my friends and me as we sat watching the hypnotic forest fire burning before us. The image is proof that someone else knows about our journey through the darkness, and somehow everything that I remember really happened. I know that it is not just my wild imagination because the picture proves that things were real.

Every Tuesday night as we go out to dinner with our friends I study each one of them to see if they show even a hint of remembering our travels together through the darkness. I laugh because as I watch each one of them, they all look guilty to me, but I cannot tell who sent me the picture.

As I glance around the table, I look at our good friends Terrell and Eddie, and I am sure that they know the true story of our journey together, because they returned our lantern that we had used all through our travels in the darkness, and when they gave it back to us they never gave us any explanation of how they got it in the first place.

Yet, as I observe Darlene and Jerry sitting smugly across from me they too seem likely to be hiding the truth. I grin as I look over at them, because I just love them so much. We have such a loyal friendship. They are two of my favorite people on earth, and of course Darlene has her mysterious green sweater, the one that matches mine, which we purchased together on our journey. Then there is my friend Bobbi who always smiles and teases like she knows something, but she won't tell. She has had a lot of heartache in the past couple of years, but she always has a smile on her face. She is my true friend. I guess it could be her, but I doubt it.

Darrell and I have our life-long friends Tom and Margaret, I smile across the table at them and they smile back. They could have sent the picture, but probably not, because I don't think they would keep a secret like that from me.

Of course there is Walt, Suzanne, Connie, Jim and Debby, but none of them really come with our group anymore. Walt and Suzanne rarely ride and Jim and Debbie have joined other riding groups and my dear friend Connie got married and moved to Oregon with her new husband.

Any one of them could have mailed me the card with the picture inside. I'm sure that one day the confusing pieces from that time in my life will fall into place and we can share the treasured memories of our trip together in search of the light. For now I just need to be grateful for their wonderful friendship.

On Saturday morning a bunch of us from our CMA group took a day ride up through Garden Valley, Lowman, and made the loop around through Idaho City and back. It was the first time that our riding group had been back up to Garden Valley together since my accident. It was a strange feeling for me to be returning to the place of such great confusion.

I remember the incidence at Garden Valley as the beginning of our travels through the day of the darkness, yet everyone else seems to only remember that I had an accident and was transported by Life Flight to Saint Alphonsus hospital.

Many different thoughts raced through my mind as we headed for Garden Valley that Saturday morning. As we traveled down the steep Horseshoe Bend Hill, I once again remembered the clutter and garbage that we had climbed through to reach the top of the mountain on our way home that first evening after the darkness began. I can recall in detail climbing around the shattered furniture, trash and broken glass. When I close my eyes I can still smell the fresh scent of hay that had been strung up and down the steep embankment after the hay truck lost control and rolled.

For one second I could see the couch and love seat standing firmly in the center of the highway after it was thrown from the Mairfield moving truck. My thoughts were so vivid I knew that they had to be true.

I was relieved when we finally got to the bottom of the steep hill and traveled on through the middle of Horseshoe Bend and out to the edge of town. As we crossed the railroad tracks I automatically glanced down the tracks to see the beautifully restored Thunder Mountain Railroad. The majestic old train was proudly parked at the railroad station waiting patiently for its next departure.

As we left town I saw the restaurant off to the right of the highway with the boardwalk surrounding the front of the building. I recalled the deserted motorcycles and cars that were abandoned in the dark parking lot as we drove in through town late that evening over a year ago.

I looked off to the left and noticed the long white familiar fence that went all the way up to the farmhouse on both sides of the lane. I clearly remember traveling down that desolate private driveway. We were in search of one small lonesome light. It was the only light that we had seen since we had left Garden Valley and the darkness occurred. But our search was in vain, because it was only a small glowing battery operated light bulb that had been left out in the farmer's workshop.

As we traveled up highway 55, every corner reminded me of the piles of wrecked vehicles that we had encountered on our way home that night; vehicles that had lost their drivers and just crashed haphazardly into each other and into the side of the mountain.

Our group turned right, off of highway 55 and headed in towards Garden Valley and I got a lump in my throat; I was not sure that I would be able to face being in Garden Valley again. I had so many confused thoughts about the incident that took place last year. Would I ever know exactly what was real and what was an enigma? I had no one to ask and no one to discuss my thoughts with about what happened. For the past year I had been forced to keep all of my opinions about this incident to myself. All I knew for sure was that the closer we got to Garden Valley the more frightened I became.

THREE

The News

We pulled into Garden Valley and parked our motorcycles up close to the outside patio dinning area, just as we had done so many times before. I took a deep breath and sat on the trike for a few moments and stared at the place that had consumed so much of my thinking for the past year. Was it the place where I had an accident or was it a place where after the blinding bright light and a loud boom the entire world had been enclosed in total darkness... or was it both? Perhaps I may never know.

As I walked up the steps with the rest of the riders, my insides began to calm down and I realized it didn't really matter which incident was real and which explanation was true. Our entire lives are made up of memories and our memories are how we personally recall things.

You can have two people that share the same event and one person remembers the event as upsetting or frightening and yet another person sees it as an exciting experience or a time of joining together. My memory of the days of the darkness and traveling with my friends was a very scary time; but it was also a time of closeness, sharing, unity, and survival.

When I honestly think about it my remembrance of that time is very comforting to me because of the close bonding with my friends.

Everyone sat down at our familiar table and instantly began to visit just as we had done so many times before. At first we looked around the patio and talked about my accident, but within a few seconds we moved on to other things.

All of us had a lot of concerns, because there were so many horrible things going on around the world. Our CMA group was close; we saw each other every week, and we knew that we all had similar beliefs about things. We often discussed the things that had been happening in the news when we got together.

CMA is a Christian organization and it was hard for us to comprehend all of the unexplainable disasters taking place in our world. It was not only the bible predictions like wars, famines and earthquakes; but it was all of the scandals. There was a new scandal on television or in the newspaper almost daily. There was so much distrust in the government, the workplace and in families that it seemed like everyone was turning against everyone else.

For almost two years there had been an alleged scandal about the numerous fraud charges that had taken place during the elections. There were people who cast write-in ballots for all of their family members, and voting machines were rigged to vote for a different candidate than the person had actually voted for.

There were scandals about Benghazi, the IRS, and the Veteran's hospitals. Our group discussed Fast and Furious, the NRA fighting for the rights of the people to keep their guns, and the wire tapping of millions of Americans.

There were whistle blowers leaving the country and people testifying in court and then being slandered and demoted and never being heard from again. The department heads would be called in under oath to testify about the scandals in their departments and they would plead the fifth and would never have to give any answers. All anyone had to say was "I heard about it at the same time you did," or "What difference does it make now" and no one was held accountable. Everyone just moved on to the next scandal.

CMA has a lot of military people, so of course we were concerned about all of the high ranking generals that had recently been demoted and removed from the military. We also talked about the Navy Seals that were used for the killing of Bin Laden; they had been sent on a mission in an old helicopter and were ambushed and taken down. No one survived. All of the bodies were cremated before they were sent home.

We read reports of groups protesting funerals and carrying signs and chanting out in front of churches as the families inside mourned the loss of their dead soldiers. At Texas A & M University, hundreds of alumni, students and soldiers lined the street in front of one of the funerals to scare off the protesters.

Motorcycle clubs from around the country also lined streets at other military funerals to show respect and to protect the families from the vicious rebellion.

Welfare and food stamp programs have soared. Our National Debt has skyrocketed and we can no longer say Merry Christmas or salute the flag in our schools. American flags are being torn down and removed from front yards because some of our NEW Americans say that the flags are offensive. Christians are being persecuted and missionaries are being killed. Chaplains are being asked not to pray in the military.

Thousands of illegal immigrant children have been brought into the United States on buses, many of them bringing with them diseases and crime. There have been numerous new cases of measles, chicken pox and mumps since their arrival. Years ago every immigrant that came to America was brought in through Ellis Island. They went through a routine process and they were all checked for infectious diseases before they were allowed to stay in the United States. Today there are no rules, once they get into the United States, they can stay here.

There is so much hatred between the black people and the white people that we are once again seeing daily riots and protests in many cities across our country. With so much anger and mistrust there has been massive looting and destruction taking place as many businesses are being gutted and burned and forced out of business.

We have all read in the newspaper about the gunman that killed two policemen as they sat quietly in their patrol car. It seems like everyone has turned against any kind of authority. There is no respect for our policemen or our firemen, and Democrats and Republicans blame each other for every situation and neither side seems to agree on anything.

Our President released a questionable prisoner in Afghanistan, Sgt. Bowe Bergdahl from Idaho. Without telling anyone else in his own government, he exchanged five well-known terrorists from Guantanamo Bay prison for Bergdahl's release. There had been a big parade planned for Bergdahl's homecoming with a huge motorcycle brigade that many of us would have attended, but there were so many threats about the way things were handled that everything was cancelled. Many soldiers from Bergdahl's unit testified that he was a deserter and that several soldiers got killed trying to find him after he left.

So much was going on right here in our own country that we couldn't believe that this was still America. We had lived here all of our lives, yet nothing seemed right.

We were disturbed about Isis and the beheadings of so many people that they had killed. We grieve over the pilot from Jordon that had been locked in a cage and burned alive. There have been mass shootings in Paris, France and many world leaders along with thousands of marchers linked arms together and marched through the streets of Paris to stand up with Paris against the terrorists.

There were 44 world leaders from all around the world, along with 1.6 million people marching in Paris, the largest group of protesters that had ever assembled there. Our government leaders did not choose to get involved, so America was not represented.

And of course, America's number one ally Israel is continually under attack, with bombings taking place every few minutes. There is evil, greed and hatred everywhere and it is hard to distinguish a friend from an enemy.

Yet, with all of the turmoil taking place in our world we can still ride our motorcycles to the mountains here in Idaho and sit safely in this open restaurant and have dinner with our friends and block out all of the problems going on around the globe. As I listened to my friends visit and share life's concerns, I had to smile because my thoughts were of thankfulness.

At least for today, we are all protected in our own safe cocoon, with our own little group, in this beautiful little mountain town. Free to pray, laugh, and visit openly about the things we cannot change.

It was summertime; time for taking long walks along the greenbelt, having barbecues, sipping lemonade with friends and having lunch with my sister and my daughters. It was time for having picnics in the park or going to the mountains or fishing up at Robie Creek. It was time for camping with friends; riding bikes and watching the kids run through the sprinkler. It was time for having homemade ice cream and playing baseball in the back yard with the kids and the grandkids.

As I glanced around the table I realized that my confused thoughts of the past were rapidly fading. I must count my blessings and stop dwelling on all of the unanswered questions of the past year and thank the Lord, for I know that I am truly blessed.

FOUR

Moving On

The next day I got ambitious and cleaned out my closet. The Saturday ride up to Garden Valley helped me to accept what was really important. I decided to throw away all of the old newspapers that I had held onto since my accident. I needed to get rid of every one of the articles that tied my thoughts together with the memories of our journey searching for the light. I no longer needed them for security. The only thing that I have left is the treasured picture with my friends that someone had mailed to me, and I keep that hidden in my dresser drawer.

I piled all of the papers in the recycle bin to be hauled away on Tuesday morning. I had looked at them for the last time and I knew that I would never look at them again. It gave me a great feeling to be able to put closure to all of my questions and doubts.

Every evening before going to bed I would call and check on our friends Suzanne and Gene, just to encourage them and to see how they were doing. They got so many things accomplished each day, we were amazed at how hard they worked. The government had declared their entire town a National Disaster area and the restoration money had been distributed within the first few days after the horrifying winds had stopped.

Our friends wasted no time getting to work. They had been working so hard and they had already replaced all of their broken windows and their front and side doors. We were astounded at their diligence. Unlike most of the other members in their community they were able to live in their basement while they put their house back together. For weeks they were the only people in their neighborhood that stayed there both day and night.

To us their property looked like it was completely destroyed, but they were never forced to leave their home and stay in Pocatello like so many of their neighbors had done.

Many of their neighbors had lost all their animals, fences, barns and corrals, so they had extra work to do to get their places back in order. Luckily, our friends didn't have any livestock. They had some chickens a couple of years ago, but a neighbor's dog killed them and they never replaced them.

Our friends were very pleased at how quickly all of the work had been done. They already had the new roof put on their house and they had several huge trees that had been cleaned up and hauled away. They both had only praise for the contractors that worked on their house. The workers had rapidly cleaned up the debris and rebuilt the destroyed areas.

Gene and Suzanne had been able to do a lot of the work without anyone else helping them, so things went much faster for them than it did for some of the other people that could not help themselves. Every night as I visited with them on the phone I could just hear the excitement in their voices as they overcame each horrendous hurdle.

FIVE

A Call from Pennsylvania

One Sunday when we were out to lunch with friends from our church we got a mysterious phone call from Dr. David Benjamin Keyes. He was the doctor that we had met at the safety location; the one who was the lead meteorological scientist from Pennsylvania. He called on my husband's cell phone. We were both trying to listen to the call at the same time, but the restaurant where we were eating was really crowded and noisy.

Dr. Keyes was almost whispering and we were having a difficult time understanding what he was saying to us. We thought he sounded upset, but we didn't know what was wrong. He told my husband he had something disturbing to discuss with us in private. The doctor stressed that it was very important and he asked if we would please call him back as soon as we got home.

Our food had just arrived for lunch so my husband promised Dr. Keyes that we would call him in an hour or so when we were home where it was quieter. After writing down the number where he could reach the doctor, my husband and Dr. Keyes both hung up.

I didn't know what to think about the strange phone call because we hadn't talked with Dr. Keyes since we left the safety location over a month ago. Darrell and I looked at each other for a second and kind of shrugged our shoulders and then went back to visiting with our friends.

We went out to lunch with these friends every Sunday after church. Oftentimes we would invite other people to go out with us, but the three main couples were Connie and Roger, Carolyn and Ron and of course Darrell and me. I had been friends with Connie for over 40 years so we knew a lot of the same people. Connie was thoughtful and caring and she had a gift of always making you feel important and that she was glad that you were there. I could trust her and she had become one of my very best friends.

The six of us had a lot in common. We shared the same religious and political beliefs, we had the same family values and we all liked cheering for the Boise State Broncos.

Like Connie, I had known Carolyn several years before we started going to church together, because we used to be in the same chapter of sorority. Carolyn was very creative, she had a beautiful house and she was always ready to open her home to all of her friends.

The six of us had so much fun together. When we got together we laughed, shared jokes and everyone loved to eat, so we always had a good time. I appreciated Ron and Roger almost as much as I did their wives.

Sunday was my favorite day of the week. Today we had two other couples with us plus a few of our single friends. We had my beautiful friend Mary and her husband, and Richard and Mary Ellen and Lou, Betty, Diane and her mother Ila Rose. It was such a blessing having a huge table full of friends.

Sometimes we would have up to 16 people in our group. It was so nice having lunch together. We always prayed and thank the Lord before we ate, then we laughed, joked with each other and just visited about nothing. Sundays were great. We loved our church and we loved our church friends.

Although we were anxious to find out why Dr. Keyes had called us at the restaurant, we leisurely finished eating our lunch and visited with our friends for several minutes before getting ready to leave.

As we walked outside to say our goodbyes a blast of hot air just kind of swooshed in through the open doors. We were overcome by the horrendous heat because it was so much hotter outside than it had been when we arrived. The extreme hot air took us all by surprise.

Roger was the first one out of the door and he gasped and commented, "Wow, when did it get so hot. I can't believe how hot it is out here. It must be 30 degrees hotter than it was earlier this morning and the sun is so bright that I can barely see." Squinting in the bright sunlight he stated, "What is going on? Even with my dark sunglasses on I can hardly focus."

Connie instantly answered him, "Me either, it is so bright and so intense, I can't see anything. It really hurts my eyes. How did it get hot so fast, it wasn't like this earlier?"

We all had to admit it was an odd kind of sunshine. It was extremely brighter than usual. The sun's glare was so radiant that our eyes wouldn't adjust, and it made the temperature feel much hotter than it really was. The heat from the sun didn't seem comforting like it usually did; the rays seemed to penetrate right through each one of us.

Mary commented, "Even the parking lot is so hot it looks like it is steaming." She was right, because as we cupped our hands over our eyebrows to shade us from the bright sun we could actually see the heat rising from the asphalt. It was so strange because it was so unbearably hot that it felt like the middle of summer after the weather had stayed hot for several days in a row. It was bizarre because it had changed so fast.

In the summer time the ground never cools down at night because it is hot 24 hours a day. Then during the heat of the day the asphalt appears to be sizzling from the sun's rays from never getting a time to cool down.

But it was way too early in the season to have the asphalt steam like this because it hadn't even been hot yet. Everything was so eerie; the hot temperature came on so quickly that the ground should not have even been warm.

Ron walked over to the front of the restaurant to look at the thermometer to check the temperature and he shouted to us, "The thermometer says it's up to 101 degrees. No wonder we feel so hot," he smiled his sheepish grin.

"It seems a lot hotter than that," Darrell commented. "The atmosphere seems really strange and the sun is a lot brighter than normal. The temperature was only in the mid 70's when we were at church. The sun now feels sweltering." He added, "It feels like we are in the middle of the Mojave Desert. For some reason the temperature has rapidly gone up within the last few hours." He got a puzzled look on his face as he went on, "In fact, I think it has changed just since we went in for lunch."

Connie and I looked at each other and slowly nodded our heads up and down in agreement. Because we knew he was right; it had only gotten hot after we went into Cracker Barrel an hour and a half ago. Our weather in Idaho changes rapidly, but not that fast.

One by one, many of the other people that had been eating in the restaurant walked out of the doors and commented on how much hotter it was than when they went in. The sun was so intense that everyone walking out of the building covered their eyes because it was so bright. They sheltered their eyes with their hands and quickly rushed to their cars.

Mary's husband had ridden his motorcycle to church and to the restaurant that day, just like he always did. Of course none of us had any idea that it would get so unbearably hot while we were in eating lunch. His motorcycle had been sitting out in the direct sunlight and it was almost too hot for him to get on.

Every one of us tried to convince him that it was too hot and too bright outside for him to ride his motorcycle home; because it was so hard to see out in the bright sunlight. But he cautiously climbed on his bike and said he would be fine. He didn't want to leave his cycle at the restaurant. He had dark glasses on and a helmet with a dark visor, and thick leather gloves to hold onto the handlebars. He rode all of the time, so he waved goodbye and slowly took off down the street. He was very cautious so he would probably be fine and he didn't have very far to go.

"This is too spooky for me," Carolyn said. "I'm heading for home where I can get out of this glaring sunlight and sit in my air conditioned house." She smiled and waved goodbye and headed towards their van. Ron then grinned and waved to all of us and followed close behind her.

Each one of us tried to laugh it off, but I felt half sick, because something very strange was going on. I have lived in Boise all of my life and the temperature never climbed this fast at one time, and I have never seen the sun so bright that you can't see anything no matter how hard you try to focus. It wasn't really the blast of hot air that was so disturbing to all of us, because it can get really hot in Idaho in the summer time. It was the blinding intense sunlight; it would soon be too unbearable to be outside.

Mary Ellen and Richard waved goodbye to everyone and quickly headed to their car. The other three ladies had left so Roger, Connie, Lou and Mary also waved goodbye and then darted to their cars and turned the car air conditioner on high.

We hopped in our car to head home, but even with our sunglasses and the darkened windshield we could barely see well enough to drive home, because the sun was so glaring.

Our house was less than a mile away, so we slowly crept home down the back roads trying desperately to see through the luminous sunshine. I worried about our friends because they had a lot further to go than we did and I knew they couldn't see in the bright sunlight either.

All the way home we could hear sirens up and down Overland Road and out on the freeway. I quietly prayed for Mary's husband on his motorcycle, but none of us had been gone from the restaurant for very long, so I was quite sure the sirens couldn't be for any of our friends.

SIX

How Could It Change So Fast

We pulled into our driveway around 2:00 in the afternoon and quickly ran to the house trying to avoid the disturbing hot sun as much as possible. As we got to the front door we saw the neighbor's little hairy puppy, Nick, whimpering on our front door step. As I opened the door he ran inside trying to get out of the blinding hot sunshine. Nick just lived next door and I knew that he would be fine in the house for a few minutes and then I could just take him home. The extreme weather had changed so quickly that it was unbearable to all of us, even the animals.

"How could the weather get hot that fast?" I asked my husband as soon as we got in the house. "And why is the sun so bright? I have never seen it quite like this before."

"I don't have any idea," he answered shaking his head back and forth. "It is bizarre how quickly the weather has changed."

Nick sprawled out quietly on the cool kitchen floor, so I just left him there. I fixed two tall glasses of ice water and closed all of the blinds to keep out the bright sunlight and then I turned up the air conditioning.

Darrell checked the outside thermometer again and I saw him cover his face with his hand as he turned around and said, "The temperature is up to 103 degrees. It has gone up 30 degrees in two hours."

"What in the world is happening?" I almost shouted out loud. "I have never seen the weather get hot this fast. I have known it to cool off rapidly when a storm comes in, but why would it be so hot? What would make the sun get so hot and so intensely blinding all of a sudden?" I questioned.

My husband continually followed the weather reports and he was like a walking encyclopedia, so I was quite sure that now that he had a few minutes to think about it, he would have some sort of answer. He said, "I think it might be a solar flare. A solar flare occurs when magnetic energy that has built up in the solar atmosphere is suddenly released."

He went on, "The sun is actually a star with energy deep in the center which gives the star its heat and shining light. The sun is just a mass of energy. The reason we are affected differently by the sun's energy is because we are so much closer to the sun than we are to other stars."

He looked worried as he bit his lip and slowly shook his head back and forth, "Anyway, I hope it is just a solar flare, because the temperature is rising surprisingly fast and I have never seen the sun shine this bright before. If that isn't it, I don't know what else it could be."

As we sat finishing our ice water we suddenly remembered our promise to call Dr. Keyes. With the odd changes in the weather we had almost forgotten that he had called. I took one of our home phones and Darrell dialed another phone with plans for both of us to hear what Dr. Keyes had to say. To our surprise his phone rang five times and then his answering machine picked up.

The recording on the other end sounded like the Doctor's voice, but Darrell dialed again just to make sure that he had dialed the number correctly. Once again the answering machine picked up on the fifth ring. This time my husband left his name and phone number so that Dr. Keyes would know that he had called him back as promised.

"That is strange that he doesn't answer," I commented. "He acted like it was an emergency when he called us at the restaurant two hours ago. He really sounded upset about something. But I wonder why he would be contacting us."

I grabbed my sunglasses and an umbrella and ran Nick next door to his house. I knew his owners were home, so I told Darrell I would be back in a few minutes.

Darrell tried to call Dr. Keyes several times throughout the afternoon, but he always got the answering machine. We knew that this was the right phone number because we checked and it was the same number that showed up on Darrell's cell phone when Dr. Keyes called him earlier at the restaurant.

All afternoon we continued to watch the thermometer as the temperature continued to slowly creep up higher and higher. By 6:00 p.m. it had peaked at 106 degrees.

As we watched the evening news we realized that the meteorologists were just as baffled by the strange heat wave as we were. They said nothing about a solar flare, and they had no other logical explanation for the weird changes in the weather. They commented that they had hundreds of calls about the blinding sunlight, but they made no clarification for that either.

It sounded like no one really knew why the weather changed so drastically. The weatherman said that things would probably cool off after the sun goes down.

The television weather announcers seemed very evasive; they kind of talked in circles and avoided telling any facts. If they really did know something about what was going on they certainly weren't going to tell any of us.

SEVEN

No One Agrees

We went to bed about 11:00 that evening and the temperature was still around 104 degrees. At 2:00 a.m. my husband got up to check the temperature and discovered it was 103 degrees; dropping only slightly from its high of 106 degrees.

At 4:30 a.m. he got out of bed again to check the temperature and to get online to see how the heat wave had affected the weather around the rest of the country.

Darrell discovered on the computer that for some uncanny reason most of the high temperature changes had started taking place in Canada within the past two weeks and then they moved on into the northwestern section of the United States.

The report stated that after traveling all across Canada the heat-wave moved into Montana, northern Idaho, Washington, Oregon, and down through California. The radical weather did not come to southwest Idaho until after it had hit all of California and was heading into Nevada. The report stated that temperatures in these states had reached frightening irregular highs within a matter of only a few hours.

The article said that the first report of the abnormal rising temperature in the United States was noted nine days ago. Extreme readings out of Canada had been reported a few days before that.

By the time the hot temperatures reached the California coast, people had become aware that something was wrong. California is known for its beautiful warm sunny temperatures, so the extreme hot weather was not a surprise to them, but the atmosphere seemed so strange that everyone could tell that something had changed overnight. It was the glaring sunlight that people were complaining about, and they were afraid to go outside. They were scared to go to the beach because the sun was too bright and the sand was too hot for them to walk on.

Within a day the entire California coastline was completely deserted. The locals were staying inside their houses and workplaces, and the tourists were not leaving their hotels. People were terrified to go outside because they didn't know what was happening, they knew something was wrong, but no one could explain what was causing the strange phenomenon. All anyone knew for sure was that the sunlight was blinding and the atmosphere had gone crazy.

After the radical weather and intense sunlight inundated all of California, it moved into Nevada and on into southwestern Idaho. Things were changing daily and the strange weather and radiant UV rays were rapidly spreading throughout the rest of America.

The article said that meteorologists were concerned because the weather seemed so out of control and they could not find any definite reasoning for the drastic changes. The weather stations had been flooded with complaints about the blinding sunshine because as soon as the temperature started to go up the sun's rays became unbearable.

No weather channels were warning the unaffected states in advance, they did not want to cause a panic by telling people to be prepared. It was not being reported that the strange weather appeared to slowly be moving across the entire United States. So, when the strange conditions came most people were taken by complete surprise, just as we were.

There was no discussion about the changing temperatures until the heat-wave actually reached their own area. None of the weather stations were allowed to tell in advance that there was an unusual occurrence that was gradually moving down from Canada.

The odd weather phenomenon was only mentioned by family members that were living in an affected area. They would tell friends and family about the strange things that were taking place in their town, but there was no explanation given for the rapid weather change, so no one expected the bizarre weather to actually engulf their own state too.

The editorial on the computer said that the most frightening part of the severe changes in the weather were the irregular UV sunrays. Once the strange heat wave envelops an area, the sun's rays become more and more intense.

The scientists are baffled by the unusually dangerous UV rays. They have no logical explanation for the disturbing intensity of the rays. They have stated that it is like the atmosphere no longer has a filter to filter out the dangerously harmful rays. But they cannot yet explain why the atmosphere would have changed so drastically to allow the dangerous rays to pass through.

The article acknowledged that one well-known group of meteorological scientists has been researching the radical weather and UV ray changes and they fear that the extreme changes have something to do with the continuous bombings taking place across the ocean in Israel. There have been continuing attacks taking place on Israel for several months and the report stated that there is a rocket fired on Israel every 6 minutes. They fear that the fall-out from the bombings is finally taking a toll on the atmospheric temperatures.

Israel has a defense system called the Iron Dome that blows the rockets into pieces before they can reach their target. The Israeli officials have stated that the system has intercepted up to 85% of the rockets fired on Israel. With that many rockets intercepted every six minutes, the scientist question what happens to all of the debris from the explosions? It has to float off into the atmosphere somewhere.

This noted group of scientists has been doing extensive research to determine where the debris from the numerous explosions is going. The scientists have been skeptical of the explosive material cluttering the atmosphere ever since they began their research over three weeks ago. After weeks of extensive testing all of their readings traced the particles directly back to Israel where all of the bombings are taking place.

They stated that the high atmospheric wind currents have caused the particles to circulate and for some unexplainable reason they seem to move towards the Mediterranean Sea and out to the Atlantic Ocean.

The team of scientists was originally sent to the Europe to track the extreme weather changes in Italy, France and Spain. Those countries were the first to be hit by the intense heat-wave and the surprising bright UV rays. It appeared that the hotter regions did not change as much in temperature as the cooler climates did. Their research found that in the hotter climates the temperature would only change about ten degrees, but it is the ultra-bright UV rays that everyone has had such a hard time coping with. The article stated that the unexplainable radical UV rays have affected over 300 million people so far.

The scientists rely on a field mode in situ observation and remote sensing equipment. In science an observatory or observable is an abstract idea that can be measured and which data can be taken. Wind profilers provide better samples both regionally and globally. A barometer measures atmospheric pressure or the pressure exerted by the weight of the earth's atmosphere about a particular location. An anemometer measures the wind speed and the direction the wind is blowing from the site where it was mounted.

After monitoring the path of the strange atmospheric changes the scientist could track the original location all the way back to the area where the bombings in Israel are being intercepted. Their equipment shows that there has to be a definite connection between the multiple bombings in Israel and the radical changes in the atmosphere and weather conditions that are taking place.

Their report states that somehow several weeks after they first started recording the extreme weather patterns that it has traveled across the Mediterranean Sea and the Atlantic Ocean and has entered Canada and is now moving down through the United States. It appears to travel faster when it is not traveling over land, because the strange weather phenomenon has crossed two oceans within only a few weeks.

Another group of scientists from Washington D.C. argued that Israel is too far away to be causing such severe weather problems in the United States. They said that we have had bombs and explosions all over the world for many years and it has never affected our weather, so why would it be causing problems now.

The scientists from Washington D.C. reminded us of what happened in 1945 when Hiroshima and Nagasaki were destroyed by the atomic bomb. They stated that the scientists at that time claimed that the radiation would last up to one thousand years and that did not happen.

Everything that the first group said the second group disagreed with and tried to discredit. The second group clearly states that the massive bombings taking place in Israel have nothing to do with the weather. The scientists from Washington D.C. stand firm on their opinion that the strange weather changes are due to global warming. They state that there can be no other explanation for the bizarre weather changes, other than global warming.

My husband sat staring at the computer and then covered his face with both hands; he seemed baffled because there was so much discrepancy about what might be causing the unusual weather patterns. He kind of mumbled out loud, "None of the scientists can agree, so what else is new? This is not scientific evidence it is just two opposite groups trying to prove that they are right." He grumbled out loud, "The only thing that they can agree on is that the unusually bright UV rays are very harmful to the eyes and to the skin. Luckily the UV rays aren't as unfiltered as they could be or we would have all burned up as soon as we walked outside."

As my husband sat at the computer digesting everything that he had just read his cell phone rang and disrupted his thoughts. "Who would be calling me at this time of the morning?" he quietly said out loud. He instantly thought of Dr. Keyes as he politely answered, "Hello." He repeated saying, "Hello," several times before the person on the other end silently hung up without saying anything.

I could hear him talking to himself from down the hall. As I groggily walked into the computer room I asked him, "What are you doing up so early?"

He told me everything that he had been following on the computer about the weather and he also read to me what both groups of scientists had stated. Then he said, "Besides, I couldn't sleep. This whole hot weather problem has really disturbed me."

As my thoughts got a little clearer I asked him, "Did your cell phone just ring?" I walked into the kitchen to check the clock and said, "What time is it?" After looking at the clock I shouted from the kitchen, "Who called you at 4:50 in the morning?"

"I have no idea. I could tell that there was someone on the line, but they didn't say anything. They waited a few seconds and then they just hung up," he said sounding confused. "I checked the number, but it says unknown."

"Well, that is weird," I said, "Maybe someone else couldn't sleep either and they just wanted to see if you were awake. It was probably one of your friends from church. Roger and Ron both get up early," I scoffed.

We go to church with Roger, but he also rides motorcycles with Darrell. Roger rides a 2003 Electric Glide Anniversary Edition Harley with a Voyager convertible trike kit. It is a gorgeous black trike with lots of extra chrome.

I hollered to my husband as I walked into the kitchen, "I'll make you some coffee. Are you staying up?"

"Yeah, coffee sounds great. This hot weather thing has really got me baffled." He said checking the outside temperature again, "It is 103 degrees and it is dark outside." He looked puzzled and said, "I wonder how hot it will get once the sun comes up and it is no longer dark?"

I looked at him and slowly shook my head back and forth without saying a word. "What would we do if it just got hotter and hotter and the temperature didn't stop going up and it got so bright that we could no longer go anywhere," I said inside of my head. "How could any of us survive?" My mind kept questioning, "How high of a temperature can people stand? Would the cars run? Could we ever go outside during the day again? Wouldn't the grass and plants all die? I wonder how much food we have. How long could we live without going to the store?"

My thoughts were interrupted when my husband shouted from the family room, "Hey, come in here and look at this. The television is talking about how hot it is in Washington. They say that the heat wave moved in about six days ago and it is already up to 115 degrees. The government has declared a state of emergency, because it has never been that hot there before and Washington is not set up for such severe conditions and no one knows what to do."

The filming of the report was from yesterday at 3:00 in the afternoon and it showed that all of the streets were completely deserted. There were no cars, buses or any people on any of the streets at all. The sun was so bright that even the photographer was having a hard time filming the segment. The reporter said that everyone was advised to stay inside during the daytime because Washington was unprepared for such extreme hot weather and the abnormal intense sunlight.

As we sat and studied the weather channel in all of the affected areas Darrell's cell phone rang again. It was still way too early for anyone to call. As he said hello over and over again the line was silent and then who ever was on the line, hung up.

"Maybe the cell towers are affected because of the strange weather," I said. "It is odd that you would get two weird calls this early in the morning."

My husband nodded his head up and down and said, "You might be right, it may have something to do with the radical heat changes from the sun's rays."

By 7:00 a.m. the sun was up and the temperature had already reached 107 degrees. Darrell tried to call Dr. Keyes again. The phone rang five times before the answering machine came on.

All throughout the day he continued to get the weird cell phone calls. Each time the phone would ring, he could tell that someone was on the line, because they would wait a few minutes and then hang up. By 6:30 that evening he had received a total of fourteen calls from the unknown phone number.

After trying to reach Dr. Keyes all day, we had just about given up that we would ever contact him. We finally decided that maybe it really wasn't as important as we first thought. We would try to contact him a few more times and then we would just wait to see if he ever called us again. We really didn't know him very well and we may never know why he called us in the first place.

EIGHT

Hot Weather

The weather continued to stay extremely hot each day, but everyone tried to keep on with their daily routines. The people of Idaho rarely let the severe heat stop them from doing things, even in the middle of the summer. It was the bright sunrays that people had to be most concerned about.

By the second day all of the water parks and public swimming pools were closed during the daylight hours and they changed all of their hours to evening hours. They started staying open until midnight every night to honor all of the season passes that had been sold. The weather remained hot 24 hours a day so it didn't really matter if it was daylight or not.

Manufacturers in California rapidly developed heavy-duty dark specialty sunglasses that completely wrapped around the face to protect the eyes so that no sunlight could filter in. They manufactured millions of specialty glasses for California and they also sent them to Oregon, Washington, Montana, Idaho and Nevada to be used whenever anyone went outside. The strange weather was gradually moving through the rest of the country, so the government stepped in and made the glasses available free to everyone that needed them.

People were warned not to go outside without wearing the special sunglasses. The glasses came in several different sizes so that they could fit large adults or small children. They also had special-made surround glasses that could be worn over regular eye glasses too. The glasses were incredibly strange looking, but many optometrists went on television stating how important it was for everyone to wear the protective glasses when they went outside.

Next everyone was advised to wear a sombrero type hat along with their strange glasses when they were out in the sunshine. The odd looking hat came in several different sizes so that they could fit every person from small children to big adults. The government gave away the large over-sized hats for people along with the glasses. Everyone was advised to stay out of the sun and never go outside without their hats or the shielding glasses on for protection.

People from all walks of life were working together to keep everyone safe. Volunteers from several church groups went out each evening and went door to door handing out the protective eye-wear and hats to make sure that every person had them. They talked to teenagers as well as the homeless living on the streets. People were scared, everyone knew that something abnormal was happening, but no one knew why and we didn't know if it would ever go away. Many people feared that life would be like this from now on.

The radiant sunlight was the worse part of the weather change. The glare was so bad that we couldn't see in the bright sunlight without the special glasses and we were continually told how dangerous it was to be outside in the daytime because of bad UV rays.

The eye doctors advised people to avoid the sun as much as possible because of the extreme UV rays. The UV rays can cause cataracts, a clouding of the natural lens of the eye; it is the part of the eye that focuses the light that we see.

It can also cause macular degeneration. It is when you damage the macula, a part of the retina at the back of the eye. High energy visibility (HEV) radiation also called "blue light" may increase your long-term risk of macular degeneration.

UV rays can also cause Pterygium, a growth on the white of the eye that may involve the cornea.

One of the things that the eye doctors warned about was corneal sunburn, or Photokeratitis which is damage to the eyes from prolonged hours exposed to the sun without proper eye protection.

The doctors advised people to not only use the proper dark sunglasses, but to always wear proper head coverage. They said to wear the hats with the wide brims to keep the entire head protected.

They told us that UV rays come from many directions. They radiate from the sun, but they are also reflected from the ground, water, snow, sand and other bright surfaces.

Because so much of the change in the weather was unclear and no one could state for sure what had caused the bright sunlight in the first place, everyone avoided being outside during the daytime as much as possible. Many organizations had changed their meeting times to evening trying to avoid people being outside during the daylight.

The one fact that all of the scientist could agree on was that depleting the ozone layer potentially could allow high-energy UVC rays to reach the earth's surface and could cause serious UV-related health problems. UVC rays have wavelengths of 100-200 nanometers. Normally, the atmospheric ozone layer blocks virtually all of the UVC rays. If it is not blocked the UVC rays can pass through the cornea and reach the retina.

As a precaution no one went outside during the brightest time of the day unless it was absolutely necessary. Everyone wore the heavy-duty dark sunglasses and hats if they needed to go out, but very few people drove around during the daytime. If they absolutely needed to go somewhere they drove directly to the location and stayed inside, and then drove straight back when they were finished.

Bacteria that cause food-borne illnesses flourish in high humidity and temperatures between 90 and 100 degrees and higher. People were advised to never keep left-over food. The health officials said to always throw away all food left out for any length of time.

Veterinarians warned people to keep their animals inside and give them lots of water. Even if your animals act like the hot temperatures do not bother them, they are not safe in the extreme heat and the unusually bright sunrays.

Emergency health reports came on the television every hour telling people to drink lots of water and other fluids, close the windows, draw the shades and crank up the air conditioners and stay inside.

Of course there were continual power surges because of the over-used air conditioners and the power was off for several minutes at a time. Many businesses closed during the brightest and hottest part of the day. People instantly changed all of their schedules and they started doing everything at night after the sun went down, so the business owners immediately changed there schedules too, so they could keep their businesses going. It was so strange because everything just automatically turned around and it was like night was now day.

NINE

Dr. Keyes

Several days after our first contact with Dr. Keyes, I received a strange phone call from him on my cell phone. I immediately apologized and told him, "We have been trying to contact you, but we have always gotten the answering machine."

He seemed very somber; I could barely recognize who it was. He talked in a low whispery voice as he began to tell me, "I'm so sorry, but there is a lot going on and I was warned to not a use that phone shortly after I first contacted you. I have reason to believe that my phone is being bugged. I have waited to contact you again until I could get on a private secured line." Dr. Keyes sounded exhausted and he talked very slow and monotone, very uncharacteristic of the way I remember him talking at the safety location. He was always jovial and upbeat even at the worst of times, but he sounded much different now. He sounded drained, worn-out, or maybe he was just scared for some reason. Whatever it was I knew that something must be seriously wrong.

I was puzzled by his odd behavior and I asked him, "Why would you be afraid to answer that phone? Why would your phone be bugged?" I talked very quietly almost in a whisper, just like he did.

Dr. Keyes paused before going on, "I am working on a very controversial weather project and things are getting rather difficult. I have been advised to use extra precautions, but I needed to contact you. I didn't know who else to call."

As I listened to the doctor talk I remembered all of the hang-ups that Darrell had received on his cell phone after Dr. Keyes had contacted him that first time. Maybe someone did bug the doctor's phone and for some reason they kept calling us after he had once contacted Darrell.

"I can't believe that someone would be tracking us down and figuring out who we were just because they were having a conflict with Dr. Keyes. What would we have to do with anything, what could anyone learn by listening to our phone conversations?" I wondered.

Dr. Keyes was silent again for several seconds trying to choose his words very carefully before continuing, "I am sorry that I had to call you, but I have been very disturbed because we got word the other day that the giant honeybees have been released over near Grangeville, Idaho."

He let out huge sigh before slowly going on, "Apparently a truck driver was just getting ready to leave the safety location the day the entomologist from Washington sent the bees through the Pneumatic transfer tube. The truck driver was the only one around when the tube arrived. He said that the transfer tube station was only a few feet from where he was getting ready to climb into the cab of his truck to head to northern Idaho."

The doctor said, "He heard the tube bang to halt and he couldn't help but pick it up to see what was inside. He noticed the unique giant bees crammed inside of a long tube. He glanced around to see if anyone came to intercept the transfer tube, but there was no one else in the cavern.

That part of the cavern was rarely used, so he knew that it might be several days before another truck entered the secured area and would find the transfer tube full of bees."

Dr. Keyes sighed, "His truck was parked in the opposite end of the safety location, on the back side of the cavern. Very few trucks entered that secured area; he was the only one that had been there that day. The entrance to that part of the mountain went down through a long tunnel and out away from where all of the destruction had been on the other side of the cavern. It was an isolated area and a difficult location to get to that is why no one ever came in through that side.

His job was to place his non-perishable delivery on the pallets at the end of the dock and sign out and leave. The delivery would be safe left alone. He never saw anyone. He just signed out and drove away. He knew that someone would pick up the delivery later and move it to the department where it needed to go.

The driver said that he knew at the time that it was wrong to take the bees, but he couldn't help himself. The giant bees would be a nice surprise to show his family and he was positive that the bees would just sit in the case and die if they were left there alone.

He thought that the bees had been sent to that location by accident and he was sure that no one would ever find them. The Pneumatic tube location was not even close to where they would be picking up his delivery off of the dock. It was on the opposite side of the cavern. He was already checked out and ready to leave, so he hid the tube in the back of his truck and just drove out of the cavern and headed for home."

The doctor sighed, "He hadn't heard anything about the giant bees taking over the wind turbines. He was just at the cavern to make a quick delivery and then he was headed back to northern Idaho. He could tell that the bees were unusual and they would be worth a lot of money because they were so large. He told me that he planned to show his family and then sell them to one of the local beekeepers."

The driver told me that he only stopped one other time to check the tube and that was in Mountain Home, Idaho. He stopped at a truck stop right off of the freeway and planned to open the tube a little to let some air in, but one of the bees tried to escape. He said he quickly slammed the end closed before any other bees could get away, but he crushed the one bee that was trying to get out. He watched the giant bee fly for a few seconds and then he saw it drop to the ground on the other side of the road. He never saw it fly up in the air again so he hopped back in his truck and drove away. He assumed it had flown across the street and died.

I gasped as I breathlessly told Dr. Keyes, "It did die; we saw that dead bee at the restaurant across from the truck stop when we were on our way home from Tower County. We were terrified when we saw a group of people looking at it, because we had no idea how it had gotten there. That is bizarre! Where are the rest of the bees now?"

Dr. Keyes went on, "Somewhere up near Grangeville, Idaho. The driver told me that the second time that he stopped; he stopped at a rest area at the top of the White Bird Summit to check on the bees. He tapped the tube, but none of the bees moved so he thought that they were all dead and that he had left them in the tube too long. When he loosened the lid to give them some air they came to life and charged him and about scared him to death." Dr. Keyes kind of chuckled, "Luckily for him they were stunned and disoriented when he let them out of the tube or he might not have been quite so fortunate. The driver dropped the tube and jumped in his truck and quickly drove away and just left the tube and all of the bees flying around at the rest stop."

He continued, "After being home for several weeks he felt guilty and contacted the city mayor, in the town close to the safety location where he had found the bees. The man was afraid that he would be arrested for stealing the unusual bees and that is why he waited so long to call."

Dr. Keyes added, "I guess his wife finally convinced him that he wouldn't get in trouble. She told him that no one really cared that much about a tube full of bees, so that's when he called the mayor's office. He knew the mayor would be able to find the owner of the bees. Of course the mayor hadn't even seen the huge bees, so he wasn't very concerned. He had heard the rumors of the giant crossbred bees being in the wind turbines, but he really didn't believe it."

The doctor paused before going on, "We all saw his town after the winds had destroyed it, so we know what he had to deal with. The mayor was too busy cleaning up after the chaos and getting everyone back into their homes. He never took the time to drive out to the wind turbines and see for himself if the giant bees were real or not. He had too much to do right in town and the wind turbines were cleaned up within a few days. I understand that they burned all of the piles of bees, so there was really nothing to see."

The community had been working day and night trying to restore their town back to normal and they have had a lot going on. The bees were not very important to the mayor; he had other things on his mind. He wasn't as concerned about what had caused all the trouble as he was about getting everything taken care of once the winds had stopped.

The mayor's secretary only contacted my department a couple of days ago. She gave me the truck driver's name and phone number and I told her that no one would be in trouble. We just needed to ask the driver some questions. I called the truck driver myself and talked with him personally."

Dr. Keyes kind of moaned before going on, "I have already contacted the three beekeepers that had worked with the bees in the wind turbines in Tower County, but none of them want to get involved. They were all three very polite, but they live too far away to travel that far again. We took care of their travel expenses before, but the government would not be paying their expenses this time. Each one of them also told me that their families would not allow them to work with the killer bees again, because it was just too dangerous."

The Doctor slowly went on, "I am getting ready to travel to Lewiston, Idaho, and I am bringing Dr. Tomlin and my wife Patty with me, but I will be there on other business. I will not be able to check on the bees."

He let out another huge sigh, "I am not sure what to do. The bees are not really my responsibility, yet I know first hand how dangerous they can be. I know what they are capable of doing if they are left on their own. We saw how rapidly they can reproduce if their environment is right."

I paused for a second before asking him, "I'm not sure exactly what you would like us to do?" I stalled for a few more seconds hoping that we could get out of this situation without being rude. Darrell and I both really liked Dr. Keyes and I knew that we should help him if at all possible because he had been so nice to us. But I really didn't want to take off on another 'Killer Bee' adventure. Except for the unusual heat-wave and blinding sunrays our life was finally getting back to some sort of normalcy.

Dr. Keyes sheepishly said, "As you know, there are very few people who even know about the giant bees. Or should I say very few people who accept the fact that there really are dangerous crossbred bees. You and your husband are two of the only people who live in the area and have actually seen them and know that they are real. Since the beekeepers won't check on them, I don't know who else to ask except you."

He kept talking, "Although I am bringing Dr. Tomlin with me and she was also there in Tower County, and she knew about the bees, we are not bee specialist either. We are coming because of the unexplainable weather changes that have occurred in the northwestern section of the United States.

Lewiston, Idaho has been chosen as a major site because it already has an extensive working weather station, and it also has a functioning safety location readily available."

Before I could answer he said, "What I really need is someone who can find the approximate location of the crossbred bees and ask some questions of the local people. Naturally, you would need to keep your distance as much as possible. We just need someone to find out if anyone has seen them and or if anyone knows where they are located so they can be taken care of."

The doctor went on, "I had checked with the State Police from that area when I first heard about the bees and there were no reports of dead animals or suspicious accidents in the region at that time."

He added, "We need someone to see exactly where the honeybees ended up and if they have caused any problems that haven't been reported yet. Once you discover the general vicinity where the bees are located, then we can get some professional exterminators from the area to help get rid of the hives."

Dr. Keyes paused, "We both know the havoc the giant bees are capable of doing, I just need to find their approximate location and then we will need to have an exterminator in that area dispose of them before they reproduce out of control."

I had to think about this for a minute, because we were not really involved in the situation. We were not beekeepers, we were not meteorologists, and we were not wind turbine specialists like Mr. Pinson. We were just innocent people who happened to be in the wrong place at the right time and ended up knowing way too much.

I sat quietly for a few seconds before finally answering, "Let me check with my husband and see what he thinks. With the hot weather like it is we would have to travel at night and I understand that Grangeville and Lewiston have been some of the most severely hit areas."

"Yes, they are two of the hottest regions. That is why I have to travel to Lewiston tomorrow. My team needs to confirm some of the research analysis concerning the extreme UV rays and temperature changes that are spreading across the U.S."

I smugly laughed, "So Lewiston, Idaho has a safety location too, just like the one inside the mountain in Tower County? You once told us that there were safety locations everywhere around the United States."

He said, "Yes, Lewiston has a safety location and it is a really nice facility. It is actually a long concrete tunnel inside the Lewiston Hill located up towards the top of "The Old Spiral Highway". It is a military run facility with armed guards stationed at the front entrance. The military uses the facility several times a year.

It is always kept on special alert, because of its location. I have actually used the facility many different times in the past five years. It has excellent weather tracking capability."

He concluded, "My team is leaving for Lewiston tomorrow around 1:00 in the afternoon. If it is alright with you, I will contact you before we leave."

I hesitated before answering, "Yes, that would be fine." I politely told my friend Dr. Keyes goodbye and promised to talk with my husband about the bees. After we hung up I covered my face with my hands and prayed, "What should we do Lord, we are just normal people trying to live normal lives. We are not heroes and we don't even pretend to be. I don't want to go to Grangeville and I don't want to worry about the giant bees again."

TEN

Time to Pack

As soon as I finished praying, a kind of peace came over me and it occurred to me that Dr. Keyes really needed our help or he wouldn't have asked us. He was right; I did know how treacherous the killer bees could be. My husband and I had seen their destruction first hand. We were among the few people who knew that the bees were real and that they were the cause of all of the devastation with the wind turbines.

If they were not destroyed, there would be no stopping them. If they were left unaccounted for, there would soon be thousands, maybe millions of the dangerous killers all throughout Idaho and far beyond our state. I knew how rapidly they reproduce. In fact, it has been several weeks since the truck driver let them go at the rest stop near Grangeville, it may already be too late. We may be searching for millions of the killer bees because they have had plenty of time to relocate.

As I was waiting for my husband to get home, I decided to go online and find out about honeybees and the hot weather. The article said that honeybees do not like extremely hot weather. In fact it said that bees are very sensitive to hot weather unless they are close to water. In hot weather bees collect water to cool their hive. If it gets too hot inside the hive the bees will crowd outside the hive on the landing and this is called 'bearding'. Bearding is when the temperature is too high, or the hive is too crowded and the bees are trying to keep from over-heating. The article said if they are near water they can withstand a lot hotter temperatures.

We had learned so much about bees in the past few months. The beekeepers once told us that the more knowledge you have about bees the safer you are. I really think that is true, because the more I read about the life cycle of the bees, the less afraid I become.

For some odd reason I do not have the terrible fear of the bees that I had before. Maybe it is because we know so much more about them than we first did. We know that they are vicious and much larger than a normal honeybee, but it is different this time. This time we know what we are fighting against. The people of Tower County had no idea what they were dealing with until it was too late. The giant crossbred bees had already taken over the wind turbines and killed several people and animals by the time anyone even knew that they existed. Dr. Keyes team would have handled things much differently if they had known in the beginning that it was killer bees in the turbines causing all of the weather changes.

As I sat there reading the article on the computer, I thought to myself, "Grangeville is only about 198 miles away from Boise, and that really isn't very far. It wouldn't take us long to drive up there and ask the local people about the bees. We could figure out their precise location and then have a specialist exterminate them. We would probably be home in three or four days." As I sat there and thought about it I realized, "There really isn't any reason for us not to help Dr. Keyes."

I shook my head back and forth and again covered my face and silently said, "I guess I should pack, I'm sure we will be going to Grangeville tomorrow."

A short time later when my husband came home from the neighbor's house I explained everything that Dr. Keyes had said to me and he agreed; we needed to pack.

We both knew that this could be very dangerous; it was not something we looked forward to doing. We just knew it was the right thing to do.

"I know that the giant bees are vicious and unpredictable; we just need to take extra precautions." I smiled to myself, "Of course, I'll see how brave I really am when we come face to face with the gigantic monsters, and they are no longer dead and lifeless and pinned to a board inside a clear glass science case like they were at the safety location."

It was almost dark, so my husband went outside and checked the tire pressure and checked the oil in the car. He wasn't sure what effect the hot weather might have on the car, but everything seemed fine. We went down to buy gas at Fred Meyer so we could be ready to go by the next evening. It was still extremely hot out, and it was dark, but at least we didn't have to deal with the over-powering bright UV rays.

When we packed our clothes we decided no matter how hot it was we needed to pack all of our leather motorcycle gear. It was the only heavy-duty clothing that we had that we could use to protect ourselves around the killer bees. We knew that the bees had taken down cattle and horses, but we couldn't think of any other clothing that we had available that would be any stronger. At least the leathers would provide us some protection and it would give us enough time to get away if we came in too close of contact with a hive of violent bees.

We didn't have the beekeeper's protective gear so our motorcycle leathers were our next best thing. We took our leather boots, our leather gloves, our jackets and pants and we also took complete protective face gear that we had used on some extremely cold trips to keep our faces covered from the weather. We were lucky that we had the leather riding gear that we could take. If we didn't ride motorcycles we wouldn't have all of the heavy-duty leathers to wear as protection, we would just be totally defenseless against the aggressive bees.

We packed flashlights, extra batteries, bee spray and our protective sunglasses from California and of course our big hats. We also took large rolls of duct tape to tape our pant legs and sleeves down when we approached the beehives. That is one of the tricks that we learned from the beekeepers when they were facing the bees in Tower County. They always taped their sleeves and pant legs to make sure there was no area exposed that the bees could get into their clothing.

Darrell packed two boxes full of food, snacks and several bottles of water and small cartons of juice; things that we knew wouldn't go bad very fast, even when the cooler no longer had ice. We took two quarts of milk for cereal and hoped it would last for at least a day. With the hot temperatures it would be difficult to keep ice in the coolers and we weren't sure what we might be able to purchase along the way. So, we prepared for the worst.

It said on the news that a lot of the local businesses in the smaller towns have been closed because of the extreme weather and bright sunlight. We are not sure if we will even be able to find gas stations, motels or any restaurants open along the way if we need them.

On the trip to Grangeville we have to climb several steep mountain areas and drive through quite a few small rural communities. The news reports said that very few people had been traveling, because of the strange weather. In fact, they had advised people to stay off of the roads as much as possible, so we were quite sure that nothing would be open if there were no people traveling through that area.

The hot temperature up near Lewiston has been the worst in the state from what the reports have said; and Grangeville is only about 70 miles from Lewiston. Our car is really good on gas in normal weather conditions so if we keep our speed down we should be able to get all the way to Grangeville and part of the way back without any problems. Of course we will buy gas at any gas station that we find open, no matter how full our tank is at the time, we will stop and top it off. We just can't take a chance on being stranded out in the hot weather.

These were strange times, there were a lot of uncertainties, and we had no idea what we might encounter on our trip in search of the killer bees. We were heading up to rural farm country and there were very few towns along the way. Plus, we will be traveling at night to avoid being out in the sunlight as much as possible, so we will most likely be all alone.

We took cereal, chips, fruit and cookies, things that wouldn't go bad very fast. Darrell and I drank coffee even in hot weather so I planned to take several thermoses full of coffee to last for at least a few days.

ELEVIN

A Promise

Early the next morning we received the call from Dr. Keyes on my cell phone. This time my husband talked with him and told him we were already packed and we would leave after the sun goes down this evening.

Dr. Keyes was so grateful that we had agreed to go find the bees. He gave my husband his private secured cell phone number and we promised to contact him as soon as we had learned anything about the bees from the local people around Grangeville.

Once again the doctor warned us, "Please be careful and do not get too close to the vicious killer bees. Do not put yourselves in danger. We just need to learn their whereabouts and then we can contact a professional exterminator in the area to destroy them. We have no plans to try to keep the giant bees alive."

He continued, "The two scientists that had been working on crossbreeding the honeybees have both been killed by the bees and I don't know of anyone else who even cares about the giant monsters. I just know we cannot let them reproduce at the rapid pace that they did in Tower County."

"Remember, even the Apiarist Franklin Faber who had developed the giant crossbred honeybees became terrified of them. After he watched them take down several large animals he feared what might happen if they were left on their own to multiple and relocate. So, once again I ask of you, please be careful," he pleaded.

Dr. Keyes said, "We should arrive in Lewiston around 10:45 tonight. We have a lay-over in Salt Lake City, Utah for about three hours, because once we get close to the affected weather area, they are not flying any planes in or out until after the sun goes down; it is not safe because the pilots have such horrible visibility with the bright UV rays. It is only a two hour flight from Salt Lake to Lewiston, but with the lay-over we will arrive late in the evening." He said, "We will be staying at the safety location up near the top of the Lewiston Hill on the old highway road. It is a very private safety location, and it is protected behind two giant metal doors. It is actually a hidden military location so it is protected by two armed guards twenty four hours a day."

After they finished talking, my husband said goodbye to the doctor and told him we would be talking to him soon. It is amazing to me how quickly a friendship reunites with some people even when you don't know the person very well. Dr. Keyes was just one of those people who instantly become one of your best friends. I looked forward to talking with him again, I was glad that we had decided to go and help him.

For the rest of the day I made several phone calls. I called all of our kids and warned them that we were going to Grangeville and would be gone for a few days. They didn't want us to go, they were afraid for us to be out in the bright sunlight and they did not want us to travel in the hot weather. I promised them that we would only travel when it was dark and we would avoid the bright UV rays as much as possible.

Darrell and I had never told our kids about the giant killer bees in Tower County, so of course we didn't mention why we were going on this trip. I doubt that our family would understand. We just said that we really needed to go to Grangeville, because we needed to help out a friend.

I called both Connie and Carolyn and told them we would not be there on Sunday for church or lunch. There had been talk of moving morning church to an evening service for awhile to avoid the bright sunlight, but either way they needed to know we would be gone. The three of us kept in pretty close contact with each other. We always tried to let somebody know if one of us would be gone for any reason. We never missed church; it was our favorite day of the week. We absolutely loved our minister and his wife; they had become two of our closest friends.

Roger was a part-time Sunday school teacher and both Ron and Carolyn and Roger and Connie were church greeters. Their job was to welcome people at the doors and give them a bulletin as they came into church.

Next I called Margaret to tell her and Tom that we were leaving town and that we may not be there for dinner Tuesday night. I also called Darlene and Jerry, I wanted them all to know that we would be traveling and to keep us their prayers.

Finally, I called Caryn, my bible study leader and told her that I would be gone and I would most likely miss bible study on Tuesday morning. As far as I knew, they were still having bible study during the daytime hours, I had not heard of any changes, but whatever they did I wanted Caryn to know that I would not be there. I have been so blessed by this bible study; it is such a great group of ladies.

After I made my calls, I washed and dried a load of clothes and got the house in order in case we were gone for awhile. It was starting to get dark out and I knew it was almost time to leave, so I made ham and cheese sandwiches for us to eat on the way.

When we were all packed and ready to go we locked up the house and went across the street and checked on Arlene and told her that we were leaving. We were quite sure we would only be gone for a few days, but just to be safe we told her that we would probably be back in a week or so.

TWELVE

On The Road

As we drove out of our neighborhood to get onto the freeway, it seemed really eerie because we didn't pass one other car. It was odd how the heat-wave controlled all of our lives. Most people stayed inside as much as possible. People that were going to work would leave for work at daybreak and return home after dark if at all possible. That is why the roads were still empty. People were not coming home from work yet. It was just beginning to get dark outside. In an hour or so there would probably be more traffic on the street as people ventured outside as it got darker.

Everyone you talked to was anxiously waiting for the heat-wave to pass and for fall to arrive so the bright sunlight would go away. Anyway, we were all praying that this strange weather would pass and it would one day be fall again. There were so many unknowns and controversial reports about the hot weather and the bright dangerous UV rays that we were not sure if it would ever go away. We didn't even know why it was here in the first place.

All we have learned so far is that the areas that have been engulfed in the strange weather phenomenon have not changed back after the region is infected. Once the temperature rises to a certain point the hot weather remains there along with the dangerous UV rays. Then the odd weather conditions just gradually move along and spread to other areas and swallow up other towns.

We drove onto Overland Road and headed for the freeway. As we pulled out onto the four-lane freeway, it too was almost deserted. There were very few passenger vehicles; it was mostly all big trucks. The truck drivers were just getting back on the road after stopping for most of the day during the bright sunlight hours.

As we merged in amongst the truck drivers, Darrell was very cautious and he kept our speed down to around 50 miles an hour because he wasn't sure what the extreme heat might do to the tires and the rest of the car after driving for any long periods of time.

The freeway never cooled down; because the weather remained so hot both day and night. We knew that most cars had never been tested to drive in such extreme temperatures for any lengths of time, so we could not judge by our owner's manual what the car could withstand.

The sun was down, but the temperature gauge in the car still read 109 degrees. Luckily we do not live in the Sahara Desert where the daytime temperatures soar to over 120 degrees and drop to 50 degrees during the nighttime. It is humidity not the heat that makes it seem hot. Relative humidity is just the measure of the amount of water vapor in the air.

Humidity refers to water in the form of invisible gas. The warmer the air the more water vapor it has in it. The reason it goes from one extreme to the other in the desert is characterized by extreme heat and dryness. A good portion of the United States is covered in forest and the forest has 80 per cent humidity that insulates the water vapor in the air. This water reflects and absorbs sunlight and the energy it brings. At night the water vapor acts like a blanket trapping heat, thus keeping our temperatures more even.

Idaho is moderately dry, but it also has a lot of dense forest throughout the state. During the heat-wave Boise has stayed around 110 to 113 degrees during the hottest part of the day and dropping to around 107 at night. Our summer weather in Idaho is hot, but it has never been as hot as it has been since the heat-wave started.

My husband and I have never traveled in such severe conditions. We are finally on our way, but it is going to be a slow, tedious, hot journey before we reach the town of Grangeville.

I looked out the window as we moved down the lonely interstate and I was amazed at how strange everything along the freeway appeared. Most businesses were lit up much brighter than normal because they were now open at night after the sun had gone down. The homes were just the opposite; they were all dark and closed up tight to keep out the unbearable heat and the radiant sunlight that occurs during the daytime.

We had traveled this freeway hundreds of times, but this time it was different. It was empty, quiet and desolate; as I glanced around at the nothingness, it was hard for me to even figure out exactly where we were, because everything looked so changed and out of place. For one quick second I felt like we were going somewhere that we had never gone before. I had to smile because I realized we were only about 18 miles away from home, it just seemed unfamiliar.

As I thought about this trip to Northern Idaho, I never once contemplated the terror of the giant bees or what we might encounter when we find them. I had never really even thought about the bees as much as I should have, I was more concerned about the exceptionally hot weather and the unexplainable bright UV rays and always being forced to drive in the dark. I feared traveling in the extreme weather and the car breaking down and getting stranded out in the middle of the night with no one else around. That's what scared me, but then I thought about the doctor and his team and how glad I was that we could once again help him and be part of his group. It felt like we were going to visit family. The more I thought about it the more pleased I was that we had decided to go to Grangeville to check on the bees.

THIRTEEN

Idaho History

As we slowly traveled down Interstate 84 heading towards Ontario, my thoughts began to wander because there was less and less for me to see out of the car window. I started thinking about the many times that we had traveled up to Grangeville and Lewiston. It is a beautiful area to visit. There is a lot of our state's history that began up in Lewiston, Idaho. I once did a research paper about that region and the narrative was fascinating.

Idaho is the 13th largest state of the United States. Lewiston, Idaho was founded in 1861 in the wake of the gold rush. It was the state's first capital of the newly created Idaho territory. The town of Lewiston is the second largest city in Northern Idaho.

Lewiston is located at the confluence of the Clearwater and Snake Rivers. Because of the dams (and their locks) on the Snake River and the Columbia River, Lewiston is reachable by some ocean-going vessels. The Port of Lewiston (Idaho's only seaport) has a distinction of being the farthest inland port east of the west coast of the United States.

The first steamboat arrived in Lewiston in May 1861. Lewiston is actually 465 river miles from the Pacific Ocean, but with the dams and locks, barges of timber and grain can readily travel from Lewiston to the ocean. Lewiston port is the lowest elevation point in Idaho at 740 feet above sea level.

In 1805, the Corps of Discovery explorers, Meriwether Lewis and William Clark were welcomed by the native people. The historical meeting led to the naming of our sister cities honoring the explorers with The Interstate Bridge that was built across the Snake River in 1945 to connect Lewiston, Idaho to Clarkston, Washington.

Lewiston's main industries are agriculture and light manufacturing. The paper and lumber products are owned and operated by the Clearwater Paper Corporation (part of the Potlatch Corporation). It is the home of the Lewis and Clark College and ammunition manufacturing also maintains a very important growing presence in Lewiston.

On the city's north end the 'Old Spiral Highway' climbs 2000 vertical feet up the Lewiston Hill. The old road is a very twisty road with 64 switchbacks and sharp curves. The road was opened in 1917 and it was the primary route for over 60 years. It ended up costing a lot more money to build than was originally planned. By the time it was completed, it doubled the initial cost estimates to more than a million dollars.

At the top of the old highway it joins together with the new US 95. The newer part of the highway was constructed in 1975 to 1977. Somewhere on the old highway is where the safety location is located, where Dr. Keyes and his team will be doing their weather research project.

Today Lewiston, Clarkston and Asotin are referred to as the gateway to the Hells Canyon. If you take a jet boat ride from Lewiston up the Snake River you eventually arrive at the Hells Canyon Dam. Hells Canyon is the deepest river gorge in North America, it is a 10-mile wide canyon located along the border of eastern Oregon, eastern Washington and western Idaho. Hells Canyon National Recreation Area has guided float trips and jet boat tours on the Snake River to take you from Lewiston to Hells Canyon and back again.

The area surrounding Hells Canyon was the home of Chief Joseph's band of Nez Perce Indians. Other tribes including the Shoshone, Bannock, Northern Paiute and Cayuse Indians were frequent visitors to the area. These tribes were drawn to the region by the relatively mild winters, lush foliage and plentiful wildlife. Today walls of the canyon are like a museum with pictographs and petroglyphs displaying evidence of the Indian's early settlements.

The Salmon River near Riggins is 425 miles long and it is the longest free flowing river in the lower 48 states. The Salmon River is also known as the **River of No Return**. It is one of the largest rivers in the Continental United States without a single dam on its mainstream.

The highest point in Idaho is Mt. Borah at 12,622 ft. and the lowest point is in Lewiston. The state of Idaho produces 72 types of precious metals. Idaho's state horse is the Appaloosa, the state fruit is the huckleberry, the state bird is the Mountain Bluebird, the state fish is the cutthroat trout and of course the state vegetable is the potato. In 1889 Lewiston was known as the 'Home of the orchids'. Idaho became the 43rd state on July 3, 1890.

Kamiah, Idaho is older than the recorded history of the west. Kamiah was the winter home of the Nez Perce Indians. They came to fish for steelhead and to manufacture "Kamia" ropes to use for fishing, hence the name Kamiah meaning the place of many rope litters. Steelhead caught in that area, have measured as much as 45 inches in length. The Nimi'ipuu (Nez Perce) have inhabited the area for thousands of years.

The Nez Perce people first obtained horses from the Shoshoni Indians in 1730. Early Nez Perce horses were considered to be high quality animals. Meriwether Lewis wrote in his journal February 15, 1806, that the horses they bred appear to be of an excellent race.

Not all of the Appaloosa horses that the Nez Perce first used were spotted. Only about 10% of the original Appaloosa horses had spots. They originally had many solid colored horses. The Nez Perce began to emphasize color in their breeding of the Appaloosa after the Lewis and Clark Expedition.

The Nez Perce peace treaty with the United States dated back to an alliance with Lewis and Clark. Lewis and Clark camped for several weeks during the early spring in the Kamiah Valley waiting for the snow to melt.

It is said that this was where the first appaloosa horse was first bred, primarily as war animals. The Appaloosa was once referred to by the settlers as the 'Palouse Horse' possibly after the Palouse River which ran through Nez Perce country. The Appaloosa horse was almost completely forgotten for 60 years. Then, it once again came to the attention of the general public in January 1937 in the "Western Horseman" magazine with an article written by Frances D. Harris, a history professor from Lewiston, Idaho. The appaloosa became the state horse of Idaho in 1975.

The Lewis and Clark expedition started on May 21, 1803 when Thomas Jefferson dispatched Lewis and Clark to find a water route across North America and to explore the uncharted west all the way to the Pacific Ocean. Jefferson thought that they would encounter wooly mammoths, active volcanoes, and mountains made out of pure salt.

Meriwether Lewis and Thomas Jefferson were long-time neighbors and family friends. Lewis was known as an outdoorsman, hunter and herbal medicine expert.

The Lewis and Clark team started upstream on the Missouri River from their St. Louis area camp. William Clark and four dozen men met up with Meriwether Lewis on a 55 foot keelboat and two smaller pirogues.

On their journey, they were told to always be on the lookout for Indians. They slept in the middle of the river, on islands whenever possible. By the end of July they had traveled 600 miles and had seen no

Indians. In August the expedition met two peaceable tribes the Oto and Missouri Indians and they exchanged gifts.

In September they met the Sioux Indians and the tribe was not very friendly. The Indians did not like the small gifts that they were given, they wanted a boat. They never really made friends with the Sioux Indians.

Only one person died on the entire expedition. Sergeant Charles H. Floyd died of an apparent appendicitis attack just west of the Mississippi. It has been reported that even if he had been in a hospital he would have died from severe complications.

One of the men that traveled with the Lewis and Clark expedition was a black slave by the name of York. York was Clark's childhood companion and devoted friend. He and his family had worked for Clark's family most of his life. When William Clark became an adult his father gave him York to have as a slave and he took his friend with him on the expedition. York was strong and very athletic. He was rarely treated like a slave; he carried a rifle and he got to vote and make decisions. He was never given wages; he performed hard labor without pay. York once saved Clark from a grizzly bear attack and he rescued him during a flood.

In October they reached the Mandan tribe's village. The Indians in the village had never seen a black man before and at the lodge the Mandan Chief tried to rub the black off of York's skin. There have been several statues built to honor York.

FOURTEEN

Sacagawea

At the village, the Lewis and Clark team built a fort to survive the 0 degree weather. That is where they hired an interpreter, Charbonneau, a French-Canadian and his Shoshoni wife Sacagawea and their baby son, Jean Baptiste.

Charbonneau's wife, Sacagawea was kidnapped by a war party of Hidatsa Indians when she was only twelve years old. She was taken from her home in Idaho to the Hidatsa-Mandan village in Bismarck, North Dakota where she was sold as a slave to Toussaint Charbonneau to be one of his two wives.

Sacagawea proved to be very valuable on the expedition because most of the Indians had never seen a white man before and Sacagawea helped them to communicate with each other. One afternoon one of the boats capsized and Sacagawea rescued many important records and journals. Clark never called her Sacagawea he nicknamed her 'Janey'. He called her Janey the entire time they were together.

The expedition exchanged gifts for favors from the Indians. When they needed horses, Clark exchanged his knife, pistol and hundreds of rounds of ammunition.

They needed horses to cross the Bitterroot Mountains and the snow was so deep that the horses almost starved to death. The men were so hungry that they resorted to eating three of the younger horses.

Clark took 6 hunters and hurried ahead to find food. On September 20, 1805 near the western end of the Lolo trail he found a small camp at the edge of the Camas-digging ground which is now called Weippe Prairie. Clark and his men were very impressed by the Nez Perce people they met.

At the camp they were helped by a small Indian boy by the name of Lawyer. Lawyer was the son of Twisted Hair. Although he was very young, he was designated to be the Head Chief of the Nez Perce tribe. The boy helped Clark and his men find good timber to make canoes. He was called the Lawyer by the fur traders because of his oratory and his ability to speak several languages.

Orofino, Idaho is the historical canoe camp where Lewis and Clark stopped to build five new dugout canoes and embarked on October 7, 1805 downstream to the Pacific Ocean.

Four miles north of Orofino is the Dworshak Dam, a concrete gravity dam. The height of the dam is 717 feet, making it the third tallest straight-axis dam in the Western Hemisphere. The dam was completed in 1973.

Orofino's climate ranks among the hottest summers and mildest winters throughout the state. On July 28, 1934 the temperature reached 118 degrees.

After Lewis and Clark reached the Pacific Ocean they waited out the winter and then returned once again through the Lewiston Valley. At one point on their returning journey Lewis and Clark separated into two groups and decided to have each group return a different way. A few months after they had gone their separate ways one of the men in Clark's group was out hunting. He shot at what he thought was an elk, but it was really Lewis clad in total buckskin clothing. The shot inflicted a lot of pain, but it was not fatal. It passed right through his left leg.

After his injury healed so that he could travel Lewis and Clark then reunited for the rest of their journey and they rode the current of the Missouri River home.

They had been gone for so long that many people feared that they had all been killed on the expedition, but they arrived home on August 12, 1806. Two years, four months and ten days after they had left. They were welcomed back home by over a thousand people and greeted with gunfire salutes.

History states that Sacagawea later had a daughter by the name of Lizette and that Clark adopted both of her children. It was written that Sacagawea died at the age of 25. There was a mix-up in the history notes with Charbonneau's second wife. Many people thought that Sacagawea lived to be 104, but it was said to be his other wife.

After the expedition was over William Clark freed his slave and friend York. York could not make it in the business world and it was written that he died trying to get back to his friend William Clark to be a slave again.

Another important historical place in Idaho's history is Wallace, Idaho. The town of Wallace has long been famous as the Silver Capital of the world with 1.2 billion ounces of silver produced in Shoshone County since 1884.

It was the only place on earth where a billion ounces of silver was mined in 100 years. Silver mining is still a big part of the economy, but today it is in total harmony with the mountain environment that attracts outdoor recreation enthusiast from around the world.

It is also known for the fact that every building is on the National Register of Historical Places. When the highway was built in 1991 the government had to go over the entire town to build the road. They were not allowed to destroy any of the buildings.

FIFTEEN

A Break

My thoughts were jolted back to reality when my husband pulled off the freeway into a quiet rest area just before Ontario, Oregon. We had decided to go all the way to Ontario and then cut across to Fruitland and Payette from Ontario. Everything was so different this trip we wanted to stay on the freeway as long as possible.

Like the freeway, the rest area too was deserted. There was only one other car in the parking lot besides ours. Even the normal travel trailers, motor homes and trucks were absent. Apparently any of the truck drivers that had waited for darkness had already moved on.

My husband pulled into one of the spaces and we cautiously looked around at the open emptiness. Everything around us has seemed so unnatural since the first day that our weather went crazy. It amazed me how quickly everything changed.

It was as if everyone just stopped living and hid away inside of the buildings. Everyone was gone. It seems like everybody is terrified of the sun. As hard as we tried to adjust, our whole life was just weird, because people were not acting normal. Our lives were turned upside down, and night had now become day and everyone cautiously did their daytime activities during the night to avoid the bright sunrays. Many people never even came out at night. They had just disappeared, and it was difficult to get used to the loneliness of the dark.

We studied the other car for a second, but we saw no movement. Apparently, the car was empty. So, we carefully got out and walked together up to the restrooms. It was hot and it was evening, and the rest area had a lot of lights glowing and it looked neat and clean just like it always did, but it still seemed odd to not have anyone else around.

We quickly used the restrooms and washed our hands then we rushed back to get into the Chrysler. When we got in the car we noticed that the other vehicle was now gone, and although we had not seen anyone else, there had to have been someone there.

The rest area was modern and well maintained so we locked our doors and decided to eat our sandwiches there in the car. We left our windows rolled down trying to circulate as much air as we possibly could for 109 degree weather.

We were almost finished with our sandwiches when an old black van roared up to the parking area and parked about 20 spaces away from where we were sitting.

A figure in a dark hooded sweatshirt instantly hopped out of the driver's side and started randomly moving from side to side as if searching for something or someone. The person bent and jerked and suddenly arched its back and covered its face as if it was in pain.

I just sat and stared out the window at the bizarre behavior of the creature in the dark hooded shirt. I sat crippled in my space silently watching as the figure moved around the grounds in front of us and clapped its hands and kind of moaned.

My husband too must have felt the strange alarm that I was feeling as we helplessly stared at the shadowy moving figure bouncing around before us. As we both intently watched the person, Darrell slowly rolled up all of the windows and reached over to start the car.

I couldn't tell if the person was a male or a female, but it was 109 degrees out, why would they have a hood pulled up over their head? All I knew was that the person was moving really jerky and that made us both nervous. It was time for us to leave.

We probably wouldn't have been frightened under normal circumstances, but there was no one else around and it seemed that nothing had been under normal circumstances lately.

Just as Darrell started the car and began to back out of the parking space to leave, the person in the hood started running towards us screaming and waving its hands and arms in the air.

Darrell automatically slammed the brake pedal and we both gasped and just stared out the front car window as the young person with the hood came towards us and fell to its knees right in front of our headlights.

With our headlights on the person's face we could then tell that the dark moving figure in the sweatshirt was that of a young girl. She was sobbing and kind of screeching as she grabbed for a half-grown golden retriever puppy that suddenly leaped into her arms and began licking her face. The crazed puppy had just come bouncing out of nowhere from the direction of the freeway. Apparently the energetic dog had run away and the disturbed young girl had been unable to find it until now. She probably feared that one of the trucks on the freeway would hit the wild puppy as it jogged haphazardly through the darkness.

After the girl regained her composure, she grabbed the dog's collar and sloppily pulled him back to the van, put him inside and then jumped in the driver's side and drove away.

"I don't think she even knew that we were sitting here," I stammered still staring in the direction of the departed van. "She just about scared me to death, but she was so worried about her dog that she never even noticed us sitting here in the car."

My husband added, "Nope, she didn't care if there was anyone else in the parking lot or not. She was completely unaware of anything around her except for her young puppy. She was only focused on saving her lost dog." My husband sighed, "Well, I am just glad she found him. I would have hated to see him out on the freeway."

I rubbed my face and quickly answered, "Oh me too, I hate to see a dog running around in traffic."

We were both still shaken and kind of embarrassed by how afraid we had been of the distraught young girl; but it seemed like everyone was nervous since the strange weather had occurred and turned everything upside down.

As we got back onto the freeway and headed towards Ontario we noticed there were a lot more cars on the road than there had been earlier. Although, it was dark and it was still very hot outside it was comforting to be in amongst people again. The night didn't seem as spooky with other people around.

Ontario was only about 60 miles from Boise, but like we planned before we left home, we would buy gas whenever we found a gas station. Darrell pulled into the first gas station that we found and filled up our tank. We knew that we would soon be leaving the security of the cities and be out on our own. The two of us would be traveling the lonely country roads heading towards Grangeville and there may not be any more gas stations available for a long time.

After we got gas, we both went inside the mini-mart and bought two large cokes with lots of ice, a bag of Fritos and a small box of powdered sugar donuts and once again we were off on our lonesome journey to Grangeville, Idaho.

As we headed out of Ontario, we turned left at the junction and then drove through Payette and on towards Weiser up highway 95. When we arrived in the town of Weiser the streets were completely deserted. We slowly traveled straight through town and quietly drove on out the other side without seeing one other vehicle or person.

Once we left Weiser we were out on the open road with no one else around and nothing to see but a few dark scattered farm houses and wide open fields.

SIXTEEN

More History

As I sat there in the darkness of the car staring out into the open meadows, I once again began thinking about our travels and the fascinating facts about Northern Idaho. In 1863 an Elk City merchant by the name of Lloyd Magruder along with four companions was murdered on a return business trip from Virginia City Montana. He had recently closed out a large stock of goods for $14,000 and was returning home. Lloyd Magruder was a well-known successful businessman and was also a candidate for congress. Magruder was murdered near the 44.2 westbound (near the Selway River).

A man by the name of Hill Beechey, proprietor of Lewiston's pioneer Luna House hotel, was determined to find the men responsible for killing his friend, Lloyd Magruder and his four companions. He told the sheriff that he prayed to God to help him capture the murderers. As he prayed he told God that he would never ask for another thing in his lifetime if only God would answer this prayer.

As Beechey followed the trail of the murderers he discovered that they had changed their names several different times. He pursued them all the way to California and eventually arrested them and brought them back to Lewiston, Idaho where they were tried, found guilty and quietly hanged. They were the first legal hangings in the Idaho Territory.

In 1980 the Magruder Road Corridor was created as a unique way for travelers to drive in the midst of the 1.2 million acre Selway-Bitterroot Wilderness area to the north and the 2-3 million acre Frank Church River of No Return Wilderness area to the south. The road is very primitive and it has changed very little since the 1930's. The Magruder Corridor winds through a vast underdeveloped area offering solitude and pristine beauty.

The 101 mile singular lane unimproved Magruder Corridor winds through the vast Nez Perce national forest. The Magruder Road is also known as the Nez Perce trail road and it is approximately 65 miles east of Grangeville.

The town of Grangeville, where we are headed is a beautiful spacious setting at the top of the White Bird Hill Summit that divides the Salmon River and the Camas Prairie. Many people originally arrived in Grangeville, Idaho in search of gold, but they stayed because they found their riches in the wonderful climate conditions and rich soil. By 1864 ranches were scattered across the prairies and along the river of the expansive Grangeville region.

The first passenger train that whistled into Grangeville was the Camas Prairie Railroad in 1908 bringing with it people, cattle, horses, sheep and swine. The Camas Prairie Railroad was an ingenious system because it had to travel over such difficult terrain.

*****

As my thoughts drifted from one thing to another, I realized we were almost to the town of Midvale. We came down the steep Midvale incline and began to glide through the town on the main highway that went directly through the center of the small darkened community.

Off to the right side of town, about a block away we could see the town's little country church with lights all aglow. It looked like every person in town was parked around the fence of the crowded community church yard. The local families had driven tractors, trucks and every type of automobile to come and meet together in the safety of that small country church. The bright lights shining through the cozy church windows gave of us a strange feeling of hope as we traveled through this lonely climate of darkness.

We continued on for several more miles before entering the quiet little city of Cambridge; it too looked dark and deserted. It was so odd driving through the once familiar rural towns, because tonight everything seemed different. We saw very few lights on and there weren't any people on the streets, in fact there was no movement of any kind. It was like everyone had just disappeared.

As we traveled on to Council, my thoughts once again drifted to the places our family liked to go visit. The town of Coeur d'Alene is named after the Coeur d'Alene people, a tribe of Native Americans who lived along the river and lakes of Northern Idaho. They lived in villages along the Coeur d'Alene, St. Joe, Clark Fork and Spokane Rivers.

The French Canadian fur traders in the 18th or early 19th century allegedly gave the tribe their native name. The non-native American name Coeur d'Alene means 'Heart of the Awal' referring to the perceived shrewdness of the trading skills exhibited by the tribe; the native language for the Coeur d'Alene people is interior Salish. Originally the entire tribe only roamed in about a 4 million acre area on the camas-prairie.

In 1870 General William T. Sherman ordered a fort constructed on the lake and named it Fort Coeur d'Alene. It was later changed to the name Fort Sherman. It is where the North Idaho College is now located.

We liked to go up to Northern Idaho at least every couple of years and go to the Silverwood Theme Park. It is a family oriented amusement park nestled up in amongst the trees with giant roller coasters, 70 rides, games, wonderful live music, a steam engine train and the Boulder Beach Water Park.

The park has a wooded camping area directly across the highway from the Amusement park. The theme park built an underground tunnel for the families to safely cross under highway 95 to enter the park facilities.

*****

One of the greatest family outings that we have ever done was to take our bicycles up to Kellogg, Idaho and ride the Hiawatha Bike Trail from Montana back to Kellogg. It is a 15 mile compacted gravel trail with a 2% grade through 8 tunnels and across 7 high old steel train trestles.

The route of the Hiawatha was also known as one of the most scenic stretches of railroad in the country. In its day the Milwaukee Railroad traveled through 11 tunnels and over nine high trestles, covering a 46-mile route that crossed the rugged Bitterroot Mountains between Idaho and Montana. The most well-known feature is the long St. Paul Pass, or the Taft Tunnel which burrows 8,771 feet (1.6 miles) under the Bitterroot Mountains to the state line.

SEVENTEEN

Stanley, Redfish Lake & Challis

Stanley, Idaho is one of the last strongholds of the Idaho frontier. It is nestled at the foot of the Sawtooth Mountains on the banks of the Salmon River.

When people in America decide to take a river float trip, they look on the internet and discover that the two most popular rivers in the United States are the Colorado River through the Grand Canyon and the spectacular middle fork of the Salmon River. Surveys have shown that if people take a river trip several different times they will only float the Grand Canyon once, but they will return time and time again to the middle fork.

The Salmon River Scenic Byway runs from Stanley to Challis on Idaho Highway 75 and from Challis to the Montana state line on US 93 through Salmon.

Redfish Lodge is at an elevation of 6,550 feet above sea level. Redfish Lake with its crystal clear water and sandy beaches is on the north shore of a glacier carved lake in the Sawtooth Mountain Range.

The resort is a wonderful place to have a family reunion. The lodge offers home style food in the dining room or you can eat in the outside gazebo.

Challis, Idaho was founded in 1878 by A. P. Challis who was the surveyor when the township was laid out. Challis has an elevation of 5,253 feet above sea level. It has a semi-arid climate with cold weather in the winter and hot weather in the summer and low precipitation throughout the year.

On Friday October 28, 1983 Challis had a significant earthquake measuring 6.9 on the Richter scale. It was originally reported as a 7.3, but it was soon corrected.

The Challis-Mackay region experienced extensive damage from the earthquake. Many buildings, businesses and homes were destroyed, but the most tragic outcome from the earthquake was the loss of two children who were just walking to school. They were killed when the front of a store fell on them.

On January 3, 2015 the area once again experienced a small quake measuring 3.7 magnitudes. That quake was felt as far away as the treasure valley about 120 miles away.

EIGHTEEN

New Meadows

It is strange how your mind shifts from one memory to another when you are driving in the darkness, in the middle of the night. We arrived in New Meadows around 1:18 in the morning. As we pulled into the junction store we discovered that it was open and the gas pumps were in service. Although it is only about 96 miles from Ontario to New Meadows, we once again filled our gas tank. We had been lucky with finding stations open and we wanted to keep our tank as full as possible so we wouldn't have to worry about having enough gas to get back home if we ran into problems.

On the second half of our trip we may not be as lucky as we have been in the beginning. There are only a few scattered remote towns along the way and much of the last part of our trip is curvy and steep and we will use a lot more gas when we start climbing. We needed to be prepared for anything.

We were making fairly good time so we decided to take a break and let the car rest for a while. Continual driving in this heat has got to be hard on any vehicle and we will soon be going up the difficult White Bird Hill Summit and we needed the car to be as cooled down as possible.

The corner store in New Meadows was the first place where we had seen lights on and other people around. We saw several people going in and out of the store before we could even finish getting our gas. The entire trip had been so intense and we both felt that this would be a good place to rest for a few minutes. It wasn't isolated and vacant like every other town that we had traveled through.

It was the middle of the night, yet there were several people in the store. It was nice to have some of the local people around to visit with. We had been traveling through the mountains and we hadn't seen any other people since we left Ontario.

As we walked into the little corner store it was like there was a party going on. Everyone was hanging out down at the store because they were unable to get out of the house during the daytime because of the dangerous UV rays. The middle of the night was the only safe time they had to congregate at the local store and discuss the situation going on around them. Everybody was coping with the blazing sunlight the best way that they knew how. The whole community was going through the same problems and they couldn't do anything to change it.

There were people sitting around on every chair, stool, bench or box. We saw people drinking coffee, coke, chocolate milk, juice and hot tea. One of the local women had made chocolate cupcakes with chocolate frosting and sprinkles and she was handing them out to anyone who was hungry. The store owner was giving away ice cream bars and serving small cups of apple juice.

Another man had purchased a large bag of Oreos and was sharing them with everyone that came into the store. It was such a pleasant atmosphere, people were laughing and telling jokes and sharing stories about their lives. Everyone seemed so relaxed and friendly even in the midst of this bizarre situation.

There were men, women, teenagers and several small children positioned within every nook and corner around the small store. People gladly moved over to another box or stool to make a place for both of us to sit down. It was amazing to see so many people out in the middle of the night. Everyone was so awake and talking and they all just acted like this was the normal thing to do at 1:30 in the morning.

As we drank hot coffee and ate Oreos and gooey chocolate cupcakes with our new friends, I casually ask the man that was handing out the Oreos, "Do you know of any beekeepers that live in this area?"

He chuckled and shook his head up and down as he answered, "Raising honeybees is very common up near the Grangeville area because of all the flowering fields. There are miles and miles of colorful fields in every direction that you look and the bees thrive on the flowering fields."

The local man never questioned why I was asking about the bees he just said, "My uncle Desmond Macy is the person to talk to about bees. He lives up near the Cottonwood turnoff just on the other side of Grangeville. He has raised hundreds of hives and he is probably the most knowledgeable person that I know when it comes to raising bees." He continued, "He also knows every beekeeper that lives in the area. He has been raising honeybees for as long as I can remember. He sells his honey to several of the local stores around northern Idaho; in fact I think they have some of his honey for sale here at the corner market."

He then went up to the clerk behind the counter and asked him for a plain piece of paper so that he could write down the uncle's address for me. As he wrote down the directions to Mr. Macy's property he reminded me once again, "If anyone knows anything about bees it would be my uncle. I know that beekeeping is a very popular hobby around that area."

We visited with our new friend for quite a while before he waved goodbye to everyone and headed home. One by one the parents with small children would leave and take their children home to bed. It was fascinating to watch all of the local people, because as one family would leave the store other neighbors would replace them and grab a cookie or a cupcake and find a spot to sit down.

It was such a welcoming atmosphere that we didn't want to leave. Every one of the people was friendly and nice. They treated us like we belonged in their community. My husband and I sat inside the cool air conditioned store for over 50 minutes and then we decided it was time for us to leave too. We needed to get back into our car and head up to White Bird; it was time for us to go and find the bees, we had put it off long enough.

As much as we dreaded leaving this jovial group of new acquaintances, it was time for us to get back on course. We were sent here on a mission and we needed to remember what our mission really was. I would have much rather stayed in the nice cool country store where it was safe and everyone was so pleasant, but my husband reminded me that we had to go find the horrifying bees.

We graciously said our goodbyes and walked outside into the atrocious heat. We had a full tank of gas and we were ready to get back into the car and head towards Riggins and the White Bird Hill.

NINETEEN

The Rest Area

We had been really lucky because we had not had any trouble with the car over-heating, but we were still taking extra precautions. Having car trouble out on the desolate highway in the middle of the night was not something we wanted to deal with. We prayed and began our long lonely journey up towards Riggins. We kept reminding ourselves that we had no choice; we had to travel at night because the sun's rays were too bright to travel during the daytime.

Darrell continually kept our speed down to around fifty miles an hour even though we passed very few vehicles on the highway. The reports on the television had been correct; there was no one else traveling, we saw only an occasional slow moving truck. We cautiously headed up to the mountains keeping a lookout for animals and wildlife of any kind.

The hot weather must have been too much for all of the animals too, because we never saw anything. Hitting animals had always been one of the dangers of driving in the dark. You had to be on the lookout for deer at all times, because normally you could not travel this stretch of the highway without seeing dead animals along the side of the road that had been hit during the night.

As we drove into the town of Riggins, we passed by several cars parked along the way and also many large semi-rigs parked on the side of the highway, but no one was driving anywhere. We were the only car that was actually moving. We could see people walking in and out of some of the local establishments, but we didn't stop. We just cautiously slowed down and went right on through and drove to the other side of the town.

After leaving Riggins, we traveled around the river and across the bridge into another time zone. Although in the middle of the night gaining an hour meant very little to us. All of the farms and houses scattered throughout the hillside seemed dark and lifeless. The whole countryside seemed serene and depressed as we headed towards the steep White Bird grade.

While silently praying and unconsciously holding my breath, we started up the abrupt White Bird Summit. I was really scared that the car would over-heat and boil over because it was so unusually hot and the incline was so treacherous. One thing about being the only people on this stretch of the highway though, you don't have to worry about passing slow moving vehicles and being forced to change lanes going up the steep slope. You can easily travel at your own speed and that seemed to help a lot.

Surprisingly the car did really well. As we approached the rest area lookout up near the top of the summit, I let out a huge sigh of relief; we had almost reached the top of the mountain without any problems.

My husband carefully pulled over into the historical lookout area to check out the surroundings where Dr. Keyes had told him to stop. Once again we were disturbingly all alone, only this time we were out of the car and standing out in the open. The entire area was void and pitch-black as we stared down into the deep valley of nothingness. I knew we were up towards the top of a steep mountain, but it was hard to get any kind of bearings because we were completely engulfed in darkness and it was so extraordinarily still. One thing about a heat-wave there is absolutely no breeze and everything is completely calm.

Even in the horrific heat, I felt a strange chill penetrate all the way to my soul, as I stared into the overwhelming darkness of the canyon below. Most likely people never stopped here in the middle of the night because it is too dark to see anything.

Dr. Keyes told us that this was the place where the truck driver had pulled over to check on the bees the day that they got away from him. He suggested that we start here first to see if there was any clue that could help us find the lost bees.

We each took a flashlight out of the backseat and began to carefully walk around the rest area checking to see if we could find anything. There were a few lights on the monuments, but it was so unbelievably quiet up on top of the mountain that it was unnatural. The absolute silence was overwhelming. The longer we stayed the more frightened I became. I wanted to get back into the car and lock all of the doors; I just wanted to leave. I couldn't stop myself, I was terrified. This whole situation was just overpowering. I was uncontrollably shaking all over, but I wouldn't tell my husband that I was so afraid, although I am sure he was really scared too. I just slowly followed close behind him pretending that everything was fine.

I continually prayed and I silently counted to ten inside of my head and forced myself to stop and read some of the big historical information signs that were all across the rim of the rest area. Reading the signs helped because I started to calm down a little.

The rest area was really nice and on a normal day there could have been hundreds of visitors stopping to read the signs, but probably not today. The two of us walked every inch of the parking area and we soon decided it had been way too long since the truck driver with the bees had been here, because we couldn't find anything.

While we were walking around searching I could hear several big semi-trucks off in the distance shifting into lower gears as they slowly crept up the steep White Bird incline. As they approached I could see the headlights of at least seven large rigs carefully lining the highway all in one long procession. They looked like the trucks that we had passed when we drove through Riggins. The drivers must have been stopped there as a group and then continued on together. I know that truck drivers constantly talk to each other on their CB's or phones so maybe a lot of them know each other.

Most truck drivers don't like to travel together because they don't all drive at the same speed, but it had to be difficult for the drivers being forced to travel during the middle of the night. They must have felt safer driving as a group and traveling together.

There is no way they could have made it up this perilous highway during the heat of the day struggling with the intense blinding sunlight. They were like us; they were forced to drive during the night and apparently they had chosen to go together.

Within a few minutes the big trucks had all reached the top of the hill where we had been searching for the bees and they sluggishly drove on by and were soon out of sight. Once again we were chillingly all alone.

After searching for almost two hours we had found no signs of the bees. The rest area was well-maintained and there wasn't even so much as a gum wrapper on the ground. We decided our search was in vain and it was time to get on into Grangeville. "Maybe the beekeeper, Mr. Macy will be able to help us when we meet him," I thought.

As we headed towards the car, Darrell stopped to take one more look around under the tables. He just couldn't accept the fact that we had stopped here and found absolutely nothing.

He shone his bright flashlight all around underneath both tables one last time and just as we were ready to leave he spotted something wedged underneath one of the concrete table legs. He had already searched under the tables two other times, but he hadn't seen the object before. He had been looking under the table from another direction and from this side he could see something. The tube apparatus was partially covered up with loose sand that was piled under the tables. Only the end of the plastic tube was visible; that is why we hadn't noticed it before.

As my husband climbed down under the concrete table slab, he couldn't believe what he was seeing, it was the pneumatic transfer tube pushed tightly under one of the concrete legs. It was about 18 inches long and 5 inches around. The tube was almost completely hidden out of sight. No one would have noticed it if they weren't looking for it, and most people probably wouldn't even know what it was if they saw it. It kind of looked like it was part of the table mounting.

The truck driver most likely threw the tube down as hard as he could when the giant honeybees started to escape from the transfer tube. I am sure the huge bees about terrified the driver to death and he didn't care where the tube ended up when he threw it. He just wanted to get out of there and get away from the bees as fast as he could. Lucky for us the tube rolled under the table and out of sight where no one else could see it.

My husband used the end of his flashlight to dig the tube away from its hiding place. As he picked it up we were surprised to see approximately ten or fifteen giant dead bees squished together in the end of the tube. The tube was partially opened and we knew that is where the rest of the bees had escaped.

As we shined our flashlights inside the long tube we determined that the remaining dead bees had probably been smothered and they were already dead when the other bees escaped. Luckily the driver had just thrown the tube down and it had rolled and was discarded out of sight.

The dead bees had not been sitting in direct sunlight or they might have been liquefied from the severe sunshine. They had been hidden in the shade of the table and the large signs so they were still recognizable.

We knew instantly that we had found what we were looking for. We had found the giant crossbred honeybees.

Even in the 109 degree weather just looking at the dead bees made me shiver. I knew that the bees had been dead for quite awhile, but I quickly closed the tube just to be safe. I shook the tube and separated the dead bees and then counted thirteen giant bees in the bottom of the tube before putting the tube away inside a white trash bag.

Darrell and I estimated that there must have been approximately 200 to 250 bees in the tube when the driver found them at the safety location. That left at least a couple of hundred bees still alive that escaped when the truck driver opened the tube that day. It has been several weeks and they reproduce so rapidly that there may be thousands of them by now.

I moaned to myself as I realized what we had to do next, "It is now our job to find the rest of the killer bees." Finding the tube with the handful of dead bees made everything real. We now knew for sure that there were hundreds of huge killer bees on the loose somewhere nearby; giant bees just waiting for us to find them, before they find us.

I shivered as I cautiously glanced around in every direction. "Where are they?" I questioned inside of my head. Being this close and not knowing where they are makes my skin crawl. I pray we have time to put on our leather gear before we meet them close up. Otherwise we'll have no protection at all.

I felt sick as I remembered the poor wind turbine worker that we saw in the hallway at the safety location. The distraught young man was screaming as he sat tied in a wheelchair after he had been attacked by the viscous killer bees. I shook my head to get the image out of my brain. "I'm not sure if the man even survived, he looked so terrible," I said to myself. "I know that the giant bees can destroy anything that gets in their way."

I exhaled a deep breath as I glanced at my watch, it was 4:24 a.m. It would soon be daylight and it was time for us to go. Finally, I could get into the car and lock all the doors, but as I slowly glanced around the dark deserted area I was not sure if the bees could actually be locked outside or not. They got into the wind turbines; I wonder if they can get into the car.

It was time to head into Grangeville and see if we could find a motel open. We needed to sleep for a while before finding Mr. Macy, the beekeeper from Cottonwood.

Grangeville was only another 20 miles or so from the rest area. As we drove into town we noticed the Super 8 motel off of the highway to the right. There were only a couple of cars in the parking lot, but the lights in the building were on. It had a vacancy sign across the registration entrance; the motel looked like it was deserted, but it said that it was open.

We turned the corner and pulled into the entrance and found a parking place and parked the car. We were so lucky to find a motel open because everything in the area looked abandoned. As we went inside, we woke up the receptionist that was asleep behind the desk. I'm sure she was not expecting anyone to come to the motel at this time of the night, especially with the terrible heat wave going on.

I told the sleepy attendant, "I'm sorry to have to wake you out of a sound sleep, but we are so glad that the motel is open. My husband and I needed to come up to Grangeville to meet someone. We wouldn't have come up here while it is so hot, but it is kind of an emergency, and of course we were forced to drive all night because the sun is too dangerous for us to travel during the daytime."

The receptionist answered, "I know, it has been like a ghost town up here ever since the horrible heat wave started. There are only four other people in the motel besides you and they have been here for six days. They came up to Grangeville for a family reunion last week, and the weather changed and they have been afraid to leave." She said, "The owner of the motel had talked about closing because of the severe weather and the unexplainable bright sunrays, but he hated to leave anyone stranded in this heat if they needed a place to stay." She went on, "We are right off of the highway and we are the only motel that has stayed open in this area."

I filled out the paperwork and got a key and then I thanked her again before heading for our room. We were exhausted by the time we unloaded our luggage and carried everything in. With the severe heat we didn't leave anything inside of the car because in a couple of hours it will be daytime and the temperature would go up even higher. I felt like I could sleep for hours, this trip had been very draining.

My husband was already snoring by the time I took a quick shower and headed for bed. I cranked up the air conditioning and climbed into the crisp clean sheets and I was out like a light.

TWENTY

The Killer Bees

I awoke with a start when I heard the loud buzzing noise coming from under the door; I knew it was the giant bees. I could hear them and I could feel them close by. Their loud buzzing; the horrendous vibrations; they were getting closer. The giant bees had come for us and there wasn't time to put on our protective leather gear, but how, how did they find us? Did they follow the scent of the dead bees? The tube with the dead bees was closed up tight, sitting on the table across the room wrapped inside a plastic bag, so how could they smell them?

The buzzing got louder. They were here. There was no time to even warn my sleeping husband. The bees had come and we were not prepared. I pulled the covers up over my face to shield my head. "Oh Lord please protect us," I instantly prayed. It would all be over soon, but what a horrible way to die. I was so terrified that I could no longer move. It was like my entire being was paralyzed. I quietly waited, afraid to make a sound.

Suddenly the buzzing stopped and the room once again became silent. I remained still. I couldn't turn from one side to the other. I listened, carefully I listened, where had they gone?

My head was clearer now and I was fully awake...it was the shower, my husband had turned off the shower and the buzzing had stopped.

Still quivering I came to my senses, "It was the shower," I said to myself. "It was not the giant bees; it was the shower that sounded like buzzing under the door."

I turned on the table lamp and sat up on the side of the bed and covered my face with my hands. I rapidly shook my head back and forth and thought, "Between the strange heat-wave, driving all night and searching for the killer bees I think I am losing my mind." I just sat there for a few minutes trying to collect my thoughts. "Maybe looking for the giant bees is getting to me more than I ever imagined that it would."

I then looked over at the clock; it was 1:22 in the afternoon. We had been asleep for almost eight hours. It was time to get up and look for Desmond Macy.

The room had a refrigerator and a microwave and we had brought food with us, so I fixed us some breakfast of cold cereal with fruit and powdered sugar donuts that we had bought at the little store yesterday. We had apple juice and I made a fresh pot of coffee with the motel coffee maker.

After getting dressed in long-sleeved clothing we grabbed our heavy-duty sunglasses and wide-brimmed hats and walked down the hall to talk with the lady at the desk. We had watched the weather reports before leaving town and knew that the weather was even hotter up in Grangeville than it was in Boise. The doctors had advised everyone to cover their entire body whenever they had to go outside; so we didn't dare leave our skin exposed to the horrible UV rays.

The same lady that we had met when we arrived early this morning was now vacuuming the lobby as we came down the hall. She turned off the vacuum and smiled when she saw us walk up to talk with her. I asked her, "Do you happen to know a man by the name of Desmond Macy? He is a local beekeeper that lives up near Cottonwood."

She shook her head and said, "No, I'm sorry I don't know that name, I have not lived in Grangeville very long. But the truck stop across the street is open and I'm sure there would be someone over there that might know him."

We told her thank you and headed for the front door. As soon as we stepped outside the heat instantly became intolerable, we could barely breathe it was so hot. The thermometer on the side of the motel read 116 degrees. The sun was so intense that I could hardly focus even with my giant hat covering my face, the heavy-duty glasses on and shielding my eyes with my hands. The glare was unbelievable.

As we tried to look around the area there was not one other person anywhere. There were no cars, trucks or any moving machinery. The motel was right off of highway 95 and yet there was no one else around.

We both stumbled blindly through the flower beds and on across the street to the large truck stop on the other side of the road. The flashing open sign on the building was on, but the parking lot was almost empty. We had stopped there many times before to buy gas and we knew they had a convenience store and a small Mexican restaurant.

Five or six people were sitting at the tables eating and just visiting when we went inside. There were no cars outside so we assumed the other people in the store must have been local people who had walked over to the truck stop just as we had.

We ordered some coffee and took it over to one of the empty tables and found a place to sit down. It was nice and cool inside the store and we could see why the neighbors nearby would congregate here.

Everyone around us was talking about the strange weather and how many of the businesses were closed until the weather got back to normal. The local people didn't treat us like strangers, they seemed glad to have us join in on the conversation. We would ask a question and several different people around the room would answer.

One of the ladies said the local companies there in Grangeville were not even opening at night. Most everything is closed indefinitely because it is so terribly hot 24 hours a day and with the intense UV rays it is too dangerous for anyone to be outside during the daytime for any length of time. Only the grocery stores and the places that absolutely have to stay open are open. The store owners say it isn't worth it to try to work, because nobody comes.

All of a sudden, the people that we had been talking to got up and left and we never got the chance to ask them about Desmond Macy. As we finished our coffee two State police officers came in all dressed in their heavy duty-sunglasses and wide-brimmed hats. Everyone in the restaurant was gone except for the gentlemen sitting at the booth next to us. Apparently, that is who the policemen had come in to talk with.

Both policemen ordered a Coke and sat down at the booth with the man sitting alone. The oldest policemen spoke first, he said, "John Bracket found two dead wolves out behind his corral a few days ago and apparently they had been dead for a several days."

The gentleman sitting at the table asked, "What killed them, the heat? Wolves are pretty tough, they will usually find shelter and burrow themselves in the ground to keep cooler and I'm sure they would stay out of the sun." The man looked puzzled, "I would be surprised if the weather got them."

The second policeman got an odd look on his face and he shook his head back and forth and glanced over at the first policeman before answering, "No they were killed by bees. The veterinarian in Lewiston did an animal autopsy and said the two wolves had large chunks of fur and hide ripped off of their backs and they were covered in huge insect bites. He said they had been attacked by large African killer bees."

The man sitting at the booth beside us said, "Bees? I have never heard of such a thing. Are you sure they were killed by bees?"

When I heard the word bees I instantly froze. I looked over at my husband and he too looked shocked. I leaned closer to him so that no one else could hear me and I whispered, "Oh no, the bees have started killing again. What are we going to do?"

Darrell shrugged his shoulders and slowly shook his head back and forth and whispered, "We need to tell them about the giant crossbred bees and find that beekeeper Desmond Macy." We started to stand up and approach the booth, but before we could do anything the men started talking again, so we sat back down and waited.

There were no walls dividing the booths, so it was easy for us to hear them talk. The first policeman was so caught up in what he was saying that he continued to talk as if we weren't sitting right next to them and could hear every word. He told them, "I know it sounds crazy, but we also got a call about an old mule that had been run to death up on the Fuller property, but we didn't pay a lot of attention to that report. We just thought that Sam Fuller had been drinking again and he found his old mule dead. We didn't really think a dead mule was a police matter so we never even went to check it out."

The second policeman kind of whispered, "Then Mrs. Murray said that her big tomcat had been missing for several days and when it came home it had huge bites taken out of its back and around its face, but it lived. She said she saw an enormous swarm of bees over near the back of her barn the day that her cat first disappeared, but the bees didn't stay very long. Within an hour they were all gone."

The policeman talking rubbed his hand across his face and kind of shook his head back and forth before saying, "But now we don't know what to think because Sam Fuller, Mrs. Murray and John Bracket only live a half a mile away from each other."

The man at the table spoke up, "Well, have you had any other reports of bees causing problems in the area?"

"Not that we know of, but with this strange heat-wave most people have not even been out on their property for awhile," one of the policeman stated.

The man at the table said, "Have you contacted Des and asked him? Desmond is the most knowledgeable bee person there is. If anything unusual is going on in the valley, he would know. He loves his bees and he has hundreds of them. He probably knows every beekeeper within a thousand mile radius."

The policeman answered, "Yes, we contacted him about an hour ago. That's why we came in here. Desmond is coming into town and he told us that he would meet us here around 2:30 this afternoon, and it is almost 2:30 now."

My husband looked at me and whispered, "Let's wait and see what Desmond Macy has to say."

TWENTY-ONE

Desmond Macy

A short time later a man in baggy overalls, a red flannel shirt, cowboy boots and a large straw cowboy hat came walking in the main entrance.

We thought the odd looking sunglasses looked strange with normal clothes, but his farming attire gave the special sunglasses a whole new appearance.

The policeman instantly stood up and motioned for the man to sit down with them, right next to us. Mr. Macy was a tall, lean man in his mid-sixties. He looked like he was a hard worker and he had a kind and gentle mannerism. He was probably very handsome in his younger days.

The first policeman shared the information about the two wolves, the cat and the old mule with Desmond Macy. Then they hesitantly ask him, "Do you know anything about some unusual dangerous bees that have entered the area?" Mr. Macy covered his face with both hands as he pondered the question for a second, but before he could answer the second policeman added, "The wolves were killed on John Brackett's property, the cat was attacked at Mrs. Murray's farm and the old mule was run to death at Sam Fuller's place."

The beekeeper got a strange look on his face as he thought for a moment about what he wanted to share, he finally said, "The Brackett, Murray and Fuller properties are right down the road from all of my beehives. I've known John Bracket, Mrs. Murray and Sam Fuller for over forty years. They are good neighbors; we have never had any trouble whatsoever."

Then we watched as Desmond Macy covered his face again with his weathered hands before going on, he looked very disturbed about something. He seemed to be having a difficult time talking. After he regained his composure he looked up and said, "Yes gentlemen, a few weeks ago some giant bees entered our area. They were several times larger than any honeybee that I have ever seen before. When they first began to invade my hives, I was excited because I thought they would produce more honey than any of my hives have ever produced before, and they did."

He shook his head back and forth as he continued, "As a beekeeper I was thrilled to welcome the huge crossbred bees. They were healthy and strong and beautiful. I was intrigued; I would just stand and stare at them for hours at a time. Within days, they rapidly reproduced thousands and thousands of the massive honeybees. I was in awe. I could not believe what I was seeing. Somehow, someone had discovered how to crossbreed these huge honeybees and I was one of the lucky beekeepers that they had come to. At first they kept to themselves and other than being several times larger than the other bees they acted like normal honeybees and they ignored my other smaller bees and just lived amongst them in their hives. They didn't seem to notice that the other honeybees were much smaller."

The beekeeper sighed and kind of paled as he once again covered his face before going on, "Then one day as I was out checking on my hives several of the new giant bees violently flew at me and just about frightened the life out of me. The new bees were a lot more aggressive than any bees I had ever encountered before. I ran to my truck and sat in the cab trembling for several minutes wondering what to do."

Mr. Macy told us, "That day, the bees just flew back to the hive once I got into my truck, but I knew there was something wrong with these giant creatures. I didn't know who to tell, because I had no idea where the bees had come from. I knew that someone had crossbred them and created them, but I didn't even know who to ask. I emailed a few beekeepers in the area, but no one else had heard anything about the crossbred bees."

He paused for several seconds to regain his composure, "I am embarrassed to say that I soon became terrified of the giant bees and I didn't know how to get rid of them."

The man continued, "I went out to my hives two other times after that. I waited for a few days and by then I had convinced myself that the bees weren't really that vicious. I had stood and watched them many times and they hadn't paid any attention to me before. I thought I had just blown everything out of proportion and for some reason I had made the bees mad the day that they flew at me." He went on, "But the next time I went out to the hives it was like they were waiting for me, and they wouldn't even allow me to get out of the truck."

He buried his face in hands for several seconds before he looked up and continued on, "It was absolutely terrifying. Within seconds after I got there a large mass of the gigantic bees absconded from the first hive and completely surrounded my truck. I could see them crawling all over my front and side windows. There were thousands of them covering my entire hood and the top of my truck. I was screaming and shouting as I put my truck in reverse and raced backwards down the driveway as fast as I could go. Finally they flew back to the hive and I precariously drove home. I sat in my driveway for over an hour trying to calm down and figure out what to do. It was one the scariest things that has ever happen to me in my life."

Desmond Macy covered his face and shook his head back and forth before going on, "I felt like I was playing a part in a horror movie and the giant bees were the lead players and they had a mind of their own. I had lost control of all of the hives, and they had just taken over. This may sound really weird, but I'm sure they were watching me." He looked up and said, "The crazy bees wouldn't even allow me to get to my other hives to check on them."

"Then the heat-wave hit. I was concerned about all of my main hives, so as soon as I got my special made sun-glasses from the store I went out again to check on my hives, but that time was the worst," he said. "As I got out of my truck, my hunting dog, Rufus jumped out of the truck and ran towards the hives like he had done so many times before."

Mr. Macy covered his face and was quiet for several seconds as he silently inhaled and exhaled a few times. When he looked up he had tears streaming down his weathered cheeks as he said, "I watched in horror as the massive swarms flew at my big hunting dog and continued to take chunks out of his hide as he ran yelping down the lane towards our house as fast as he could go. The bees followed him for several minutes before the heat got to them and they were forced to return to their hive."

He continued, "I searched for over an hour before I found my trembling bird dog laying in the stream a mile up the road. He had huge welts covering most of his back and head where the bees had taken bites out of his thick coat. I know that the bees would have killed him if they were not forced to return to their hive because of the heat."

The disturbed beekeeper quietly stated, "The vet says that my dog should make a full recovery, but many of the chunks were so great that he had to have stitches. The vet also said that the hair around the deepest wounds will most likely grow back in a different color, because the wounds are so large and so severe. I'm not sure if Rufus will ever be the same again, because he was so traumatized, but at least he is alive."

I couldn't sit still and listen any longer; it was time for me to tell them about the killer bees. I stood up and went over to their booth and introduced myself and said, "Excuse me, but we couldn't help but overhear what you were saying about the giant bees. My husband and I were sent here to locate the giant crossbred bees that you are talking about. That's why we are in Grangeville. We got word that they were released up near the White Bird Summit rest area and we were asked to come and find their exact location so that they can be destroyed."

It wasn't until everyone introduced themselves that we discovered the man sitting at the table next to us, was the mayor of Grangeville. That is why the policemen had been discussing the giant killer bees with him.

The mayor then invited us to sit down with them and tell them where the huge bees had come from. For the next two hours my husband and I told our story about how the Apiarist Mr. Faber in American Falls had crossbred and developed the giant bees. We told them how the bees had turned on him and how they had killed his horses and his goat. Then they eventually killed Mr. Faber and his wife before moving into the wind turbines in American Falls.

As I told them how the bees had also killed many cows, some antelope and the entomologist from Washington, my husband walked back across the street to the motel to get the tube of bees that we had found at the rest area. I shared with them how the entomologist from Washington had transferred a queen and her drones in the pneumatic transfer tube. I told them how the truck driver had found the tube at the safety location and had stolen it and brought it up to this area before letting them escape. Once again I cautioned them at how extremely dangerous the bees were and that Mr. Macy had every right to be afraid of them.

When my husband returned with the tube of bees, we placed several of the large monsters out on a paper plate, so that we could all get a better look at them. No one could believe how large they were. It was hard to believe that they had once been alive.

The older policeman frantically said, "What can we do to destroy them? From what Desmond tells us they are multiplying so fast there will soon be no way to stop them. It may already be too late."

Desmond Macy calmly spoke up again and said, "One thing that I know, honeybees do not like hot weather. In fact a normal honeybee does not do well in weather this severe. The stream is close by, so they have water and that helps honeybees when the temperature gets really hot."

He said, "I think we should all go out after it gets dark and see how well the bees have done in this heat-wave. With the darkness and the hot temperature the bees will be more dormant at that time and we should be able to get close enough to check on them."

He shrugged his shoulders and kind of lowered his head before saying, "I have been afraid to go out and check on the hives by myself. I know that it is very dangerous, but I would feel safer if I were not alone."

Every one of us looked at each other and reluctantly nodded our heads up and down stating that we would go out with him.

The beekeeper went on, "Of course these are a different breed of bees and I'm not sure what they will do in this relentless weather. They may be stronger than normal bees because they are not normal; they have been crossbred to be hardier. They are vicious and much larger and from what I can tell, they don't do anything like normal honeybees from normal hives. They reproduce at an accelerated pace and they seem to be unusually cunning and watchful." He kind of smirked and said, "Most honeybees just keep to themselves and continually pollinate the fields and create honeycombs the way God intended them to do."

Mr. Macy again shook his head back and forth, "I'm sorry guys, but when man messes with the normal cycle of life, things get all messed up. We have had a real problem in the past few years with what is called

'Colony Collapse Disorder' in the beehives. Bees have been dying off in droves since the mid-1990s."

He told us, "First it started in France and then it came to the United States. Colonies have been mysteriously collapsing and the adult bees are disappearing and abandoning their hives. Honeybees are the most economically important pollinators in the world. Out of 100 crops that provide 90% of the world's food, over 70 of those crops are pollinated by bees; valued at over $19 billion dollars."

He went on, "Seven in ten biologists believe that losing the honeybee is more of a problem than the threat of global warming. The beekeepers just wake up one morning and all of the bees have disappeared and we never see them again. I am sure that is the reason that the scientist have tried to create a new stronger species of honeybees; they are trying to stop the 'Colony Collapse Disorder' in the hives."

TWENTY-TWO

Facing the Killer Bees

We all decided to leave for a few hours and collect our things and meet back at the truck stop at 8:00 tonight. It gets dark earlier up in Grangeville and so it should be almost dark by then. We told them that when we came back this evening we would bring our own car. The plan was for us to follow the State Police car and the mayor and to meet Mr. Macy out near the beehives.

After saying our goodbyes we walked back across the street and paid for the room for another night and then went back upstairs to get our gear in order for later. After getting everything ready we watched television for awhile and discovered that the heat-wave had moved down through Utah, Wyoming and a large percentage of Colorado. It seemed to be spreading to other states rather than going away. We had seen enough so we turned off the television and decide to rest for a couple of hours until it was time to put on our leathers and go out and meet the bees.

At around 6:30 we got dressed in our leather riding gear and drove across the street to the truck stop to get something to eat before it was time to meet up with everyone else. We grabbed a sandwich, chips and some coffee in the convenience store and sat down to eat them before the two policemen and the mayor arrived. This would be our only chance for any type of dinner.

Before the police and the mayor arrived, we taped our sleeves and pant legs with the duct tape so that the bees could not creep inside of our leather clothing during a confrontation. Just the thought of trying to fight off the violent bees seemed crazy to me. What were the policemen going to do; shoot them? Obviously, Mr. Macy couldn't protect us. He couldn't even protect himself. The more I thought about the situation the more terrified I became.

At 7:52 the State police car pulled into the parking lot and close behind was the mayor and one of his neighbors, a man named Mr. Riley.

We nodded to both the mayor and the policemen and they nodded back as we climbed into our car to go out to meet Mr. Macy and the giant bees. We had no idea where we were going, so we made sure to follow close behind. Everyone else knew exactly where the bees were located, but we didn't. It was easy to keep up because there were very few cars on the highway.

There seemed to be quite a few more people outside walking around since it had gotten dark, but it was still relatively quiet. Except for the lady in the motel, we hadn't seen anyone else, only the mayor, the two policemen, Mr. Macy and the people in the truck stop since we arrived in Grangeville. It seemed strange to have other people around. We had been in our own little world ever since we arrived in Grangeville early that morning.

The longer we were in the car the more nervous I became. I felt queasy. I couldn't believe we were going to meet the killer bees face to face. "What have we gotten ourselves into?" I questioned inside my head. I wanted to turn around and race back to Boise, but it was too late for that.

We were off to greet the dangerous crossbred bees and there was no turning back.

Within a few miles the police car put on their turn signal to turn left and we spotted Desmond Macy's old truck a short ways up ahead. My heart was pounding and I could barely breathe as we turned down the lane where the honeybees were housed. This was the same lane where the bees had killed two wolves, run an old mule to death, attacked a large cat and tried to kill a big hunting dog. I was sick. The road was just an old country dirt road used by the local neighbors to get to and from their small farms, but tonight it seemed like an ominous passageway from a nightmare.

It was almost dark by the time we reached the place where the beehives were stored. We could see boxes and boxes of beehives every direction that we looked. Mr. Macy must have had hundreds of beehives because they seemed to be everywhere. My hands were shaking so badly I could hardly turn the handle to open the door to get out. Somehow the door opened and I was forced to step out into the frightening hot air.

Darrell and I put on our heavy-duty face masks, helmets and leather gloves as the seven of us stood back and just stared in the direction of the hives trying to collect our thoughts. We needed to have some sort of plan, but we really didn't have one. The only thing that we knew for sure was if the bees started chasing us, we could not outrun the deadly swarm, especially Mr. Macy with his beekeeping attire, and my husband and me with our heavy leather boots, helmets and leather gear.

As I glanced over at the beekeeper and then at my husband I couldn't help but smile at the way we looked. I said to myself, "What a scary army we must look like in our helmets, facemasks and our heavy leather motorcycle gear. It is a sweltering 112 degrees outside and we are all dressed in our mismatched militia fighting outfits ready to take on an army of killer bees. I hope the bees don't laugh themselves to death."

Of course, poor Mr. Macy didn't look much better in his wide-brimmed beekeepers hat, his monk-like garment and armed only with a smoker for a weapon. This whole situation might have been funny if it wasn't so real."

Mr. Macy had also taped his pant legs as well as his jacket sleeves just as we had. He motioned for the two policemen to stand far back along with the mayor and his neighbor Mr. Riley.

He then motioned for my husband and me to stay close behind him and he once again whispered to assure us, "The bees are always quieter at this time of the day and perhaps the three of us can calmly see how many bees we are dealing with before we get the exterminators out here. They have reproduced so rapidly it might take several exterminators to dispose of every one of the killer bees."

The beekeeper had already gotten the smoker out of the back of his truck to use to calm the bees down in case of an attack. He put his hand to his face and whispered for us to not make a sound and then he waved us forward to go and face the bees. No matter how frightened we were, it was time to move and the only weapon we had was a bee smoker.

We had been told in Mr. Faber's notes at the safety location that smoke did not work on these giant bees, but we said nothing to Mr. Macy because we hoped that it would work for him. It was all that we had. I had heard that it usually worked to calm bees down, so I silently prayed that it did this time.

As I watched Mr. Macy I became more frightened because he was a professional beekeeper and he looked petrified. I really felt sorry for him; he seemed like such a sweet man and yet he was the only one that could take care of this horrendous situation. He had already been chased by the massive swarms and he knew that these were not normal honeybees. They truly were killers.

With giant flashlights in hand we cautiously approached the beehives. The closer we got the more frightened I became, I was shaking uncontrollably. My flashlight was moving in every direction and I couldn't keep it steady. I silently prayed, and somehow I kept moving forward. As we approached the first hive it was deathly silent. We heard absolutely nothing; the bees were even quieter than Mr. Macy had described.

Desmond Macy turned on the smoker and with his hands violently shaking he pointed his flashlight towards the first hive. The beehive was alarmingly mute. As he cautiously approached the tranquil hive he let out a huge gasp. Surrounding the outside landing were hundreds of dead honeybee parts. We could see masses of the giant crossbred bees as well as the normal sized honeybees, but every bee was dead and cut in half.

After looking inside the first hive he motioned for us to follow him to the second box and once again each bee was dissected. There were thousands of tiny bodies snapped in half. In every beehive we saw piles and piles of cut up bees, and we didn't find one live bee in any of the hives. Every single bee had been cut in half. The bees that were cut up around the landing were 'bearding.' They were on the outside of the hive trying to stay cool, but they too were all dead and chopped in half.

Beehive after beehive we searched and we found thousands and thousands of dead bees both giant killer bees and every one of Mr. Macy's priceless honeybees; but all of them had been killed.

We cautiously walked from hive to hive and when we were sure that all of the bees were dead Desmond Macy motioned for the two policemen and the mayor and his friend Mr. Riley to come up with their flashlights and look at the hives themselves. After all of the hives were checked again the beekeeper went to his truck and got several cardboard boxes and he started pouring the dead bee parts into the large boxes for him to examine at home.

"What has happened here?" I whispered to my husband. "It can't be the heat because heat does not dismantle its tiny victims."

"I don't know, this is uncanny," he quietly answered me. "Well, at least we found the giant killer bees like Dr. Keyes had asked us to do."

The mayor solemnly asked the beekeeper, "I don't understand, what has happened here? What cut the honeybees into little pieces?"

Mr. Macy thought for a second before answering and he said, "I'm not sure, but I think they may have been ambushed by wasps. Wasps can stand a lot hotter weather and they will rob the honey from the hives, but they will also eat the bees or at least cut them into pieces, depending on what type of wasp it is. A wasp has strong sharp mouth parts that can effortlessly cut a bee in half."

He went on, "This has been a very bountiful year for wasps and with the horrendous heat they could easily watch the honeybees and take advantage of their weakness to the weather. Wasps have always been a problem for the honeybees, but they are worse this year because of the heat-wave. With the heat they could easily overpower the bees and they are merciless; they would not give up until they have mutilated every bee in every hive. An invasion of hungry wasps can be enough to wipe out entire colonies. They see bees as furry and lovely and the wasp is a vicious creature."

Although we were all in shock we helped Mr. Macy put the smoker and the boxes in the back of his truck. Every one of us just stood there in the darkness and stared at the eerie hives in disbelief. We weren't sure what we needed to do, we felt so confused because everything had gone differently than we had expected it to go.

It was finished and there was really no reason for us to stay around here any longer. The problem of the bees was over. Every one of us seemed baffled by what we had seen. We all just stood there in the darkness and stared at the hives for a few more seconds until each one of us slowly turned around and walked back to our cars in complete bewilderment.

Standing at the vehicles we said our goodbyes and made plans to meet at 9:00 a.m. the next morning at the truck stop across the street from our motel. That would give Mr. Macy time to sift through some of the tiny bee body parts and decide for sure what had happened to all of the bees.

Darrell and I anxiously drove back to our motel. We could hardly wait to get out our hot leather riding clothes. The nighttime temperature had now dropped to 110 degrees, but it was far from feeling cool enough to wear leather from head to toe. We were lucky to have our motorcycle gear as extra protection if we had needed it, but thank the Lord we will never have to find out if it was enough protection to save us from the bees or not.

As we traveled back to our motel, I had very mixed emotions and I felt really bad for Desmond Macy because he had lost every one of his honeybees. I told my husband, "This entire evening has just been unreal. I cannot believe that we were so terrified and yet all of the bees were already dead and the horrifying nightmare was already over when we got there, but we just didn't know it." I looked at my husband and laughed, "Now all we have to worry about is the horrendous heat-wave and the unsafe UV rays and always having to drive in the dark."

He looked over at me and kind of groaned, "Well at least our life is never dull."

TWENTY-THREE

Answers

The next morning we ate a light breakfast in our motel room and left our luggage there where it would stay cool. We once again put on our weird heavy-duty sunglasses and our big goofy hats and headed across the street to meet the mayor, Mr. Macy and the two State policemen. We ordered coffee and sat down in the same booth that we had been to before.

At exactly 9:00 a.m., Desmond Macy and the mayor arrived. Mr. Macy got a cup of coffee and the mayor bought a large orange juice and brought it over to the table. Within a few minutes the state police car pulled up and our two new police friends walked into the truck stop. The policemen ordered coffee and donuts and then they came over to the table and sat down where the rest of us were sitting.

There were no other people in the restaurant at that time so we were at liberty to talk openly. Mr. Macy spoke up first and he said, "The bees were definitely killed by an attack of the wasps."

He continued, "Last night after I got home and sorted through the broken bee parts I came to the conclusion that they had been chopped up and killed by wasps. I contacted fifteen other beekeepers from around the area and ask them to go out and check on their hives. When they each called me back we discovered that every single beehive has been invaded by the wasps, every honeybee in the valley has been destroyed."

He went on "I am not alone. Every person that I talked to also lost all of their hives. When they went out and checked on the hives they too found their beehives were filled with mutilated body parts."

He told us, "All of the beekeepers in the valley are close friends and we often help each other out when someone has a problem. We decided that we will need to start over with fresh new hives as soon as the heat-wave passes. We will have to order the new bees from a long ways away, someplace that has not been affected by the hot weather." He shook his head back and forth and kind of shrugged his shoulders and said, "We are all set up and all we have to do is clean out the cluttered hives full of dead bees and purchase the new bees and start all over again. They have been destroyed by wasps not by any kind of disease, so the hives are still usable."

 Mr. Macy smiled and told us, "Thank you for going with me last night to check on the hives." He looked at the mayor and smiled before going on, "We all really appreciate you coming up to Grangeville in search of the bees, because we know you didn't really have to come here. You were just here helping a friend."

He smiled and said, "You helped us to know what we were up against and where the bees had come from and how they got up here in the first place." He looked at my husband and said, "I was so discouraged after the bees got my dog I didn't know what I was going to do. I couldn't just walk away and leave them there to multiply and hurt everyone that came near them."

He continued, "It was such a terrible feeling having the deadly killer bees out at my hives and being too afraid to go out there and face them. It was easier just to stay away and hide from them. I was just sick worrying about what I was going to do. After they attacked my dog I was really angry, but there was still nothing I could do to stop them."

He nodded his head up and down and grinned, "At least we know for sure that the bees have been destroyed, and even if I did lose all of my own bees and I am forced to start over with all new hives it really helps me to know that I am not in this situation alone. All of the beekeepers in the valley have to start over too and we are all here to help each other."

He shook his head back and forth again and slid his right hand across his face and he got really serious before going on, "You know this may sound strange, but I have been so anxious about those giant bees it is almost worth it to me to lose all of my own bees just to get rid of them. This last couple of weeks has been a nightmare for me and my wife."

He then stood up and said, "I have something for you guys." He walked over to the front of the store and picked up a small box that he had been carrying earlier. He handed me the small container and when I opened the lid I discovered that it was filled with multitudes of broken pieces of the giant crossbred honeybees that he had sifted through the night before. There must have been a total of five hundred bees in the container that he had prepared for us.

He told us, "I brought these for you so that you can show them to the doctor that sent you here to Grangeville. You will have proof that you found the bees and that every one of the killer bees has been destroyed. Of course, I did not bring you all of the dead bees because I have thousands of giant bees mixed in with the regular bees just in the boxes that I have at home, but this should be evidence enough," he grinned.

"Thank you," I told him. "That is a great idea. I would like to study the bees up close again myself. I remember seeing them inside the glass container at the safety location and I was stunned. They were so beautiful; it was hard to believe that they could be so vicious."

My husband added, "I will be honest with you, I promised Dr. Keyes I would come up here to find out where the bees were located, but I had no idea what I would do with them once we found them."

My husband laughed, "I'm really not sure who is more pleased to find all of the bees dead, you or us. My wife and I both dreaded coming up here to locate the killer crossbred bees, because we knew how deadly and destructive they could be. We were terrified to get involved, but we knew we had to come. For us the entire situation couldn't have ended up any better."

TWENTY-FOUR

Let's Celebrate

The mayor then smiled and began to speak, "I have talked to several people on the phone this morning and we would really like to invite you to a dinner this evening. My friend Mr. Riley, the man that you met last night has a restaurant on Main Street and he wanted to plan a town gathering so that you could talk to the local people. Maybe you could answer any questions that people might have about the giant bees.

My husband quickly answered, "Believe me, I am not an expert on bees." He laughed, "I just came to check on the bees for our friend because no one else would do it. I only knew about the giant bees in the first place because I was in the wrong place at the right time."

I smiled as I politely replied, "Of course we will come to dinner, we will be glad to."

Everyone said goodbye and then we took our box of bees and walked back across the street to the motel to tell the person at the registration desk that we would need to save our room for the rest of the day. We planned to leave tonight after the dinner was over, and once again travel in the dark and head up to Lewiston.

We had settled the problem with the giant bees so rapidly that we decided to take the box of bees that Mr. Macy had given us up to the safety location and show them to Dr. Keyes and his team. The doctor told us approximately where the safety location is located so we felt sure we would be able to find it. Lewiston is only another 70 miles up the road from Grangeville. We can make it in about an hour or two, because the highway is good and it is fast traveling. We have been on it many times.

The first thing we did when we got back to our room was to study the giant bees in the box that Mr. Macy had given us. It was fascinating sifting through the box of bees and to realize that these dead mutilated creatures could cause so much damage and then to be taken down by wasps. It was amazing to think that a tiny insect like a wasp could actually cut a giant honeybee like these in half, but we could see that they did.

We were so pleased that we had been given the box full of crossbred honeybees to take to Dr. Keyes. Along with the dead bees that were inside the pneumatic transfer tube that we had found at the rest area we would have quite a lot to show Dr. Keyes and his team. It was a good feeling being able to help him solve at least one of his problems. We could tell by talking with him on the phone that he had a lot on his mind.

After we had studied the bees for awhile we closed up the box and slept for a few hours. After we had rested, we got in the car and drove across the street to fill the car with gas. Once again we had been lucky with finding stations open, but we didn't want to take any chances. We needed to make sure that our tank was always full. Most likely there will be many stations open in Lewiston because it is a larger city, but with the horrible heat we couldn't be certain. We had heard that the heat-wave is even worse in Lewiston.

Around 7:30 we headed down Main Street to have dinner with a few of the local people in town. We found the restaurant easily because it was just a few blocks away from our motel and it was right on the main street just as the mayor had said. When we pulled into the back parking lot of the restaurant we were shocked because the entire place was packed with cars and people from town and the surrounding area.

We walked inside with many of the local farmers and town merchants. Everyone seemed to know each other and they talked, shook hands and patted each other on the back. There were old farmers in their work clothes and ladies dressed in designer jeans. It was an interesting mix of people, and we were surprised at how crowded the room was. There were people standing around everywhere.

The restaurant had prepared a wonderful buffet for everyone. The people of the town were all paying for their dinner, but they refused to let us pay, because they said that we were the guests of honor. My husband and I were starved because we had only eaten sandwiches and snack foods for the past several days. After we ate dinner, we talked with the local people for over three hours. The mayor was right; the townspeople had a lot of questions.

Desmond Macy had a tray with the giant dissected bees along with 3 of the whole bees from the pneumatic tube, placed on a table in the middle of the room so that everyone could actually see what we had been up against. All fifteen of the beekeepers that he had talked with on the phone, along with their families were there to visit with us.

We soon discovered that none of the other beekeepers had been invaded by the giant bees. The crossbred honeybees had only entered Mr. Macy's hives and so we were encouraged that all of the deadly bees had truly been destroyed.

After the beekeepers had time to talk to each other and analyze the situation it was decided that Mr. Macy's beehives were the closest hives to the area where the truck driver had let the bees escape. He also has the largest number of hives and that would attract the giant bees to his beehives. That is why all of the killer bees settled in his hives.

It was interesting to listen to the beekeepers talk the situation over. They all seemed to be such kind, honest people, and you could tell that they really were good friends with each other. They discussed many theories as to why the bees only bothered Mr. Macy's hives. They all seemed genuinely saddened by his horrendous loss, because out of all of the beekeepers he had lost the most. The beekeepers stated that Desmond lost at least ten times more bees as any of the other beekeepers did.

It was encouraging to listen to the men talk, because none of them were willing to give up. They each promised that once the heat-wave was over they would rebuild their beehives again. They all knew how important honeybees were for pollination and they planned to help each other start new hives when it was time to start over.

My husband and I shared stories about the giant killer bees with everyone. We told them of the severe problems that the bees had created when they took over the wind turbines in Tower County, stories that we had never shared with anyone else before now. But these people could see for themselves that the giant crossbred bees were real, because the dead bees were spread out on the table in front of them.

It was finally time for us to tell the truth about all of the destruction that the bees had caused and how the bees were created and crossbred on a farm near Pocatello, Idaho. It was time to tell people what we knew. The bees could never harm anyone again. Besides, we had never been asked to lie about the bees in the first place. We just never told anyone before now.

There was a lady there from the local newspaper and a man asking questions from the local television station. They took several pictures of the giant bees and a lot of snapshots of the local people standing around the room. They talked with the mayor of course and then Desmond Macy shared his fears and told them about the attack on his big hunting dog.

Everyone seemed extremely grateful that the nightmare of the giant bees was taken care of, but they couldn't get over the brutal problems that might have happened if the heat-wave had not come and the wasps had not been able to destroy all of the giant bees.

The people of Grangeville had never even heard of the giant crossbred bees before today. Word of the killer bees in the wind turbines had never reached this far north because the giant bees were never talked about on the news, not even in their own area. For us it was kind of a relief to be able to tell the truth about the bees; we were tired of keeping the truth from everyone and pretending that we hadn't seen anything.

Darrell and I really enjoyed talking with everyone, and we were glad that we had stayed in town for the dinner. Although we were not bee specialists, we had a lot of answers to their questions because of our involvement in Tower County. There would be no more hiding the truth about the bees. The secret of the giant crossbred killer bees was now out because the town of Grangeville had thousands of dissected bees as proof.

We were having a great time visiting, but as soon as the people started going home we decided it was time for us to leave too. We tried not to act like we were in a rush to leave, but we were anxious to get headed up to Lewiston. It was getting late and we still had several hours of traveling ahead of us in the dark. We wanted to find the safety location before sunrise.

We said our goodbyes to our new friend the mayor, the two state police officers and of course Mr. Macy. We told Bill Riley and his wife Lisa what a wonderful job they had done on the dinner and then we headed back to our motel to get our things and to check out of our room. We quickly packed the car and headed off towards Lewiston, Idaho to find Dr. Keyes and his team.

TWENTY-FIVE

Highway 95

We got back onto highway 95 and headed towards Cottonwood and Lewiston. When we first got on the highway we passed a few trucks and an occasional car; at least were not completely alone this time.

The longer we traveled the hotter it got, even for the middle of the night the temperature was still going up. We had been on the highway for over two hours when the temperature hit a frightening 117 degrees. Keeping our speed down to thirty five miles an hour seemed to be taking us forever to get there, but we felt it was safer because of the unknown weather conditions. We were probably only about twenty miles out of Lewiston, but the closer we got to town the hotter it became. It was 2:40 in the morning and yet our temperature gauge was still rising.

It was eerie traveling in this abnormal heat. We had no idea if the car could keep driving in temperatures this hot or not. It was so frightening I could hardly breathe; I was sitting on the edge of my seat. All I could do was silently pray. The air conditioning was keeping the car inside cool, but the temperature was so extremely high outside we weren't sure if we should even have the air conditioner on in the car. I could hardly wait to get to Lewiston and find a safe place to stop. It was so scary driving in this horrendous temperature we didn't know what to do.

Darrell continued to keep our speed down, but knowing that the temperature was continually rising was mind provoking. We had never been anywhere before when the weather was this hot, and we had no idea how high the temperature would continue to go.

Suddenly, I realized we were once again all alone; everywhere I looked it was dark and there was no one else around. "Have you noticed that we haven't passed one other truck or car for over a half an hour?" I said to my husband. "We saw a few other people on the highway when we first left Grangeville, but there has not been anyone else around for several minutes."

He answered, "Yes, I have noticed that. I have been checking my rearview mirror and there has been no one behind us for a long time. There are no other headlights in sight, and we have not even passed any large trucks for over an hour. This is the time of night that the trucks should be driving too, because with these hot temperatures they wouldn't dare try to travel in the daytime," he replied. "I am really surprised we haven't seen anyone else, because we will soon be to Lewiston and I expected to see a lot more traffic the closer we got to town."

Suddenly as we came around a sharp curve we could see why we hadn't passed any other cars for awhile. Lights were flashing everywhere and the highway was completely blocked off. We carefully pulled over to the side of the road and got out of the car. The abnormal heat instantly overpowered us as we cautiously walked towards the accident.

There were two large semi-trucks sprawled across the highway blocking both directions. Apparently, the weight of their load was too much for the truck tires in this heat. Several of the tires had burst and there were tire parts scattered for hundreds of feet in every direction.

There were three police cars, and an ambulance already at the scene. It appeared that both drivers were stunned, but they were alright because they were up and walking around. The ambulance attendant was occasionally giving them oxygen and then the drivers would go off and walk around again, but they seemed disoriented.

The heat was absolutely unbearable. It was hard to breathe because the air was heavy. As we stood there dripping in sweat a giant tow truck arrived to move the two large semi-trucks out of the way. "We would all need oxygen if we didn't soon get back into the air conditioning in our cars," I thought to myself.

As the tow truck went to work, Darrell and I walked back and got into the car. The heat was too much for us to tolerate. I thought to myself, "I don't know what we will do if the air conditioner stops working in the car. No wonder no one else drives very far, they are afraid of being stranded somewhere."

Within a few minutes the tow truck had moved the giant trucks out of one lane so that we could at least pass by. We had waited at the accident long enough that there were three other cars and one semi-truck lined up behind us.

Slowly we got through the wreckage and we were once again on our way and heading towards Lewiston. But after seeing the frightening accident with the truck tires splattered about the highway we slowed down to thirty miles an hour, we were afraid to go any faster. We weren't going to take any chances.

Apparently seeing the big trucks lying on their sides must have frightened everyone behind us too, because not one person passed us. They just cautiously followed us all the way into Lewiston at thirty miles an hour. We were glad that the people behind us stayed with us, we were grateful for the company. It seemed that nobody wanted to be alone on the road. It was safer driving together.

The temperature dropped one degree as our small convoy drove in beside the river. When we entered the Lewiston city limits the temperature was 116 degrees because of the river, but it would soon be daylight and the temperature would then go back up to who knows what.

We drove along the river for a few miles until we saw a sign that told us how to get to the "Old Spiral Highway." As we turned off to follow the sign our faithful friends in the vehicles behind us continued on straight ahead, and we were once again traveling alone.

TWENTY-SIX

The Old Spiral Highway

Darrell followed the signs to the north end of town until we came to the old highway. The crooked old road looked very intimidating as we slowly approached the beginning of our climb. The entire area seemed deserted; there was no one else around, so we took a deep breathe and started up the steep neglected old road hoping to find Dr. Keyes. We knew that we couldn't get lost, because there was nowhere else to go.

The sun would soon be up and the temperature was starting to rise again. We needed to quickly find Dr. Keyes and his team, because climbing this ghastly hill in this heat was a hardship on the car to say the least. We slowly crept around one sharp curve after another. The car was literally hill climbing it was so slow and tedious. It was obvious that very few vehicles ever came up this road. Darrell and I had driven up this twisted highway once before with a motorcycle group, but we have never attempted it in a car until now.

The higher we climbed the hotter the temperature rose outside and the gauge for our car's engine began to change. For the first time since we left home our radiator was about to boil over and there was nothing we could do to stop it. We quickly turned off the air conditioner and rolled down the windows and turned the heater up on high in hopes that we could buy a little more time before the engine quit.

Higher and higher we climbed, and except for an occasional barn or outbuilding there was nothing on the old highway that looked like a place for the safety location. We were positive that we hadn't missed it, because we were watching so closely, but we were almost to the top of the mountain and we hadn't seen anything yet.

I closed my eyes and fervently prayed, because towards the top of the hill the temperature had reached 119 degrees and the sun began creeping up over the hilltop. We would soon be forced to put on our special sunglasses or we will not be able to see anything. If the car boils over and stops running we will be stranded up here all alone on top of the hill with nowhere to hide and no protection from the violent sunrays.

My husband hadn't said a word; he just solemnly stared straight ahead; reverently looking for any kind of landing that might be the safety location. I'm sure he was terrified too, but he just kept driving with his eyes focused on the surrounding area up ahead, hoping that any minute we will find what we are looking for.

I was trembling at the thought of the car breaking down and to keep from screaming out loud, I began to silently yell at myself inside of my head, "What are we doing up here on the top of this inferno? This is crazy. The kids were right; we have no business traveling in this horrible heat-wave with the unforgivable UV rays. I can't believe it, we are about to die up here on the top of the old Lewiston highway and no one even knows that we are up here. Between the strange weather and the fact that this road is abandoned they may not find us until next winter."

I felt angry at myself for giving up so easily and feeling so defeated. I closed my eyes and once again I began to pray. I hated the feeling of being so hopeless. I couldn't believe that we had come all this way for nothing. We had taken care of the killer bees, but if something happens to us no one will ever know that they were destroyed.

I shouted at myself, "How could we have missed a giant tunnel? We were almost to the top of the hill and we have not seen anything." All of a sudden as we came around one of the last corners before reaching the top of the mountain we spotted a small gravel landing off to the left side of the road. We probably would have never noticed the landing if we had not been anxiously searching for it, and it was easier to see because it was starting to get light outside.

The area around the landing looked abandoned just like the rest of the old neglected road, but as we pulled up into the driveway we could see that it was actually a deep pathway set far back away from the steep road. It could not easily be seen from the old highway. We both let out a huge sigh of relief, because we knew that we had found the obscured safety location.

As we slowly crept up the dusty path we followed the road around a small mound until we came upon two massive iron doors that looked completely out of place for the side of a mountain. The doors could not be seen from the old highway. You had to drive around the pathway several hundred feet and face the other side of the mountain to find them.

If Dr. Keyes had not told us about the pathway that led to the giant doors we would have never known that they were up here. The doors were so well-hidden that I doubt that they could even be seen from the air, because they seemed protected and surrounded by the sides of the mountain. The whole concept of the giant doors and the hidden tunnel was absolutely amazing. The military had a magic way of creating concealed safety locations that looked almost invisible to the ordinary person, and this location was no exception.

We were told that there were armed guards positioned somewhere behind a large metal structure, but we couldn't see them. We wouldn't have known that they were there if Dr. Keyes had not warned us of their presence ahead of time. The guards remained hidden completely out of site as we approached.

Little by little we continued to make our way up towards the giant doors. As we got almost to the entrance one of the guards hollered to us from a loud speaker demanding that we stop. Without leaving the safety of the metal cover he asked us, "What are you doing up here."

My husband loudly told the guard his name and then shouted back "We have come to see Dr. Keyes and his team."

The guard apparently radioed to someone behind the metal doors because within a few minutes the giant doors began to gradually open and the guard motioned for us to drive through.

We entered the massive entrance to the tunnel and drove into the cave like structure. The tunnel was enormous. It was like something out of a science fiction movie. It was absolutely inconceivable that this massive tunnel was located up here in the side of the mountain, right above Lewiston, Idaho.

A soldier in a small Army Jeep was there to go before us to show us where we needed to park our car. We parked our car over against a long wall where several other vehicles were already parked.

The soldier politely suggested that we get what we needed out of our car and put it in the Jeep and he would then take us to see Dr. Keyes. We each grabbed a small travel bag and put them in the back of the Jeep. Darrell went back to the car and collected all of the bees to show them to the doctor.

It was so much cooler inside the safety location than it was outside. It was probably fifty degrees cooler in the tunnel. It was such a relief. I wanted to just lie back in the seat of the Jeep and close my eyes and breathe. I could not believe that we had made it to the top of the mountain and were safely inside the safety location.

It was only a couple of days ago that we had first talked with Dr. Keyes on the phone and so much had happened since our last conversation. The doctor will be surprised because we have already taken care of the bees and we are up here to show him what we have found. The entire situation is incredible. It seemed like our whole life had become one big adventure novel over the past couple of years. We never know what we will be doing next.

TWENTY-SEVEN

The Tunnel

I motioned for my husband to sit in the front seat, next to the driver and I gladly climbed in the back of the Jeep and leaned my head back against the seat. I often sit in the backseat of the car and have my husband sit up front with the driver. It never bothered me one bit to sit in the back seat of a car and let him sit up front to visit with the driver, especially if the driver was another man.

I closed my eyes for a second and thought, "It is such a relief to be out of the heat I never want to go back outside again. I hate the hot weather." I smiled at the thought, "Couldn't we just live here in the tunnel for the next few months until the weather cools off outside and then maybe go home for Christmas?"

I finally came to my senses and I began to look around, I started studying the inside of the enormous cavern as we rode along. Driving through the tunnel in the Jeep was amazing. The tunnel was a giant cave like structure cut deep inside of the mountain. It looked like it was completely manmade because the ceiling, walls and floor were solid concrete. The ceiling was approximately fourteen feet high and the tunnel was at least thirty feet across and as we looked up ahead it seemed the pathway went on for miles. It was extremely long and it was so deep that we could not see the end of the tunnel from where we were riding.

There were lights that were placed along the top of the tunnel approximately every 100 feet. The tunnel was so straight that it looked like an endless subway leading to nowhere. It was neat and clean and I could tell that it was continually maintained. It would probably be very claustrophobic if there were not so many lights to light the way. In fact it was a little overwhelming to think that we were actually traveling inside a giant cement tunnel, deep inside of a mountain. It was a mountain that we have driven over many, many times on our way to northern Idaho. But it was totally different being inside the mountain than it was traveling seventy miles an hour down the wide Lewiston Hill grade with its four run-away truck ramps.

As I looked around at this incredible structure I once again questioned inside of my head, "I wonder just how many other tunnels and safety locations are located up in the sides of the mountains."

We traveled through the tunnel for several minutes until we came to a doorway off to the right of the main passageway. As we approached the opening we could see bright lights streaming through the wide entrance. When we began to turn to the right we could also see lights shining in from the other side of the tunnel. The doorway seemed to be some sort of an intersection to go to other parts of the cavern.

As we reached the bright opening the driver turned to the right and headed directly into the new passageway. This tunnel was somewhat smaller than the main tunnel, but it too was long and well lit. It also had concrete walls, a concrete floor and a concrete ceiling.

We traveled along the second roadway for several more minutes, continually driving us deeper and deeper into the core of the famous Lewiston Hill. The massive tunnel was unbelievable.

In a short while we came to another opening that turned to the left, this tunnel was identical to the tunnel that we had just been in. Only this time we seemed to slope down at a strange angle. Down, down, down we traveled deep inside the huge inner core of the mountain. We were quickly dropping down, going deeper and deeper inside the middle of the giant mount. The deeper we dropped the cooler the air became; until I almost felt chilled.

"Where are we going?" I screamed inside of my head as I sat up in the seat for a better look. This was starting to get unsettling. All of a sudden, I panicked and I changed my mind about staying until Christmas. I wanted to turn around and go back the way that we had just come in. I felt like running, but where would I run to? I knew that the only thing back at the entrance was the intolerable heat-wave and the unforgiving UV rays, but I was having a difficult time adjusting to being so deep inside of a mountain.

Everything had happened so fast. We just entered the tunnel through the giant doors and jumped into the Jeep and took off racing towards the center of the mountain. We couldn't help but feel vulnerable; the whole situation was a little overpowering.

As I looked up at the driver, he did not seem alarmed. When he realized I was staring at him, he just graciously turned around and looked back at me and smiled a friendly smile and simply said, "We're almost there." He must have sensed that I had concerns.

I had become more and more fretful the deeper inside of the mountain that we went. I was so uneasy that I could barely talk, but I knew that I should answer. I finally just shook my head up and down and smiled back at the driver and said, "Great."

I was hoping that I wouldn't start hyperventilating and pass out from feeling like I was buried deep inside of a tomb. Rapidly traveling down a passageway to get to the inside core of a mountain was something frighteningly new for my husband and me. Everything seemed to be racing out of control. All we could do was hold on and wait to find out where we were going.

Within a few seconds we came upon a massive glassed-in opening and the driver pulled up near the window and stopped. The driver was so nice he must have known that I was struggling with being so deep inside of the mountain. He politely said, "I'm sorry ma'am, I should have warned you that we would be so far underground, but I didn't realize that you had never been here before. Most new people have a difficult time when they realize that they are so deep inside of a mountain, but trust me you'll get used to it. By tomorrow you will probably be right at home."

I couldn't help but feel better, because the young man had such a comforting smile. He was the type of person that you just instantly trusted. He had a strong southern accent and I was impressed by his true concern; he was sensitive enough to take the time to try to calm our fears.

We got out of the Jeep and the polite military man helped us get our bags from the back. Darrell grabbed the box of honeybees and then stepped away for the young man to leave. As I courteously smiled and told him thank you, I had to silently laugh because I realized I must have looked terrified if he felt he needed to apologize to me for bringing me down to the interior of the mountain.

Just as we finished talking to the driver, a door opened up next to the big window and Dr. Keyes and Dr. Tomlin came out to greet us. Close behind Dr. Keyes was a pretty blonde lady that he introduced to us as his wife Patty. We were so glad to see our friends again and they were smiling and they seemed genuinely pleased to see us too.

My husband spoke up first and said, "We have found the bees and you will be glad to know that they are all dead. We have a box full of the dead bees that we brought to show you," he said with a proud smile across his face.

Dr. Keyes seemed shocked, but very relieved. He patted my husband on the back and motioned for everyone to follow him into another chamber of the tunnel. We all waved goodbye to the young driver as he drove away and then we followed the doctor into the metal doorway.

As Dr. Keyes talked to my husband, I realized how pale the doctor looked. He had big dark circles under his eyes and he looked as if he hadn't slept for several days. Our gracious friend looked like he was carrying the weight of the world on his shoulders. I could tell by watching him that something was drastically wrong.

We followed the doctor into a large office area and he motioned for each of us to find a chair and sit down. The office was large and cheerful and very well-lit for being in the center of a mountain. It was decorated with bright colors and there were a number of multi-colored office chairs placed around the room. There were enough chairs for each one of us to sit down and comfortably visit around the desk.

The office was surrounded by floor to ceiling windows that looked out into a massive weather laboratory. Like the lab in Tower County this location also had gigantic surround screens monitoring the weather changes, but these screens were different than the limited screens in Tower County. This laboratory was showing the weather information all over the entire United State and several other countries all around the world. It continually changed screen segments every few minutes. Many of the images changed more quickly showing the temperatures in several different locations throughout the United States at the same time.

One screen showed a chart with some sort of ratings that graded the UV sunrays as they continually affected different locations all around the world. Each screen had one technician posted at the screen monitoring a minute by minute chart showing the severe changes and tracking the severity of the dangerous ultra-violet rays.

It was fascinating that they could track so many areas at one time. Many of the locations posted were hundreds of miles away from Idaho.

With such sophisticated equipment, it looked like they could track most of the world from here in this one laboratory. There were technicians in blue jumpsuits following the odd weather phenomenon from every angle of the screens.

We studied the many complex weather monitors as they scanned the individual problems, and the more we watched the more we realized that we had no idea what was going on. This severe weather situation was completely beyond our comprehension, but as we watched the technicians at work it appeared to be a mystery to them too.

No wonder Dr. Keyes looked so exhausted, the United States was rapidly being destroyed by the extremely hot weather and severe sunrays and it is up to him to find a solution for the problem. But just by watching his demeanor we were quite sure that he hadn't found a solution yet, and he didn't know what to do.

Even with all of the extensive equipment he did not seem to be finding the solution to fix the shocking unstable weather. As we watched the giant screens, we witnessed the heat-wave as it continued to spread throughout our country. The involved areas were being marked off in yellow, and even as we watched more and more yellow markings appeared on the charts.

As my husband stood by the window and stared at the weather screens he asked Dr. Keyes to tell him about the mammoth tunnel. He said, "I am fascinated with this tunnel. What was this tunnel originally built for?"

As always, the doctor was very open and honest about his situation at the safety location. He told us, "The tunnel is all manmade and all of the walls, floors and ceilings are eight feet thick and made of solid concrete. They needed to be thick enough to withstand earthquakes, storms and bombings if ever necessary. The tunnel was the perfect model for a bomb shelter of the late 1970's." He went on, "It was constructed in 1976 at the same time the new Lewiston Hill highway was being built."

He told us, "The project was all top secret and it was constructed literally unnoticed because of the construction of the new highway. It was developed as a secluded military operations project, because the entrance is not easily seen from the air or the road."

He continued, "They developed the idea of a tunnel because it is practical, solid and it is large enough to transport an entire Army unit all the way through the mountain and into Northern Idaho and almost all the way to Canada without being ambushed or even seen. Naturally, the deeper inside of the mountain that you travel, the safer you are from any enemy."

The government needed a safety location in this region of Idaho that would be an ideal place to hide a large military unit or a visiting dignitary or President because it is naturally isolated and cannot be easily penetrated or destroyed.

The tunnel is large enough for an entire unit of tanks to go all of the way through Northern Idaho without ever being out in the open. The tunnel is several miles long and has a number of smaller tunnels going off from the main tunnel."

The safety location is completely self-contained. It has its own water, sewage and power system. It even has it own private climate controlled air and heating facility and it has a food supply to feed two hundred people for seven years. It has sleeping capabilities to accommodate several hundred people for a short while if it is ever needed.

He added, "The tunnel project took almost three years to complete, but it gets used many times each year as a hidden military training base. The military enters from the upper end of the old highway, always coming in from the new highway connector rather than driving up the steep, twisted old road. In fact the old Lewiston Hill highway is rarely used anymore."

He told us, "I have always marveled at the concept of the tunnel. To think of how they build a cement tunnel that goes straight through the middle of a mountain, and cannot be seen or traced from the air is absolutely brilliant. There is not another safety location like it anywhere in the United States. Several years ago they tried to construct a similar facility in Wyoming, but it was never completed."

Dr. Keyes smiled and said, "The weather laboratory where we are now is actually located in the middle of the mountain. That is the safest place for the security of our global weather equipment. We can track the weather from any part of the world from this one secluded location, and we are actually fifteen hundred feet inside of the mountain."

Dr. Keyes told us, "The tunnel is a combination of man's sophisticated architecture with the architecture of a mountain created by God. It is constructed out of concrete and it is isolated and protected by the strength of the mountain. When the tunnel was first built it was said that it could withstand the strongest earthquake and the most powerful bomb created because of the natural depth and consistency of the mountain."

He smiled, "Much of the bulk of the mountain was discovered to be solid rock. When they were building the new highway they found that a large portion of the mountain was very difficult to even chisel away with dynamite. That is why the tunnel is so deep down inside of the mountain, because the deeper area was an easier area for them to dig out to build the tunnel.

After he had answered all of my husband questions he smiled and said, "Now tell me about the giant bees." Dr. Keyes motioned for my husband to sit down near to him as he took his seat behind the desk.

My husband reached for the box of bees and then picked up the pneumatic transfer tube of dead bees that we had found at the rest area. The doctor looked astonished as he stared at the box of giant dissected dead killer bees. I'm sure he was startled to find the huge bees all cut in half.

When Dr. Keyes finally spoke he questioned, "But how, how did you destroy these huge creatures?" He looked even more puzzled and asked, "Why did you cut them up into little pieces?"

My husband laughed, "We didn't cut them up. They were invaded by wasps, and the wasps mutilated every single one of them. In fact with this horrible heat-wave the wasps actually destroyed every honeybee for miles around."

Darrell told him how he had first discovered the pneumatic tube buried under the concrete table up at the rest area. He said that we had searched for several hours until he spotted it hidden beside one of the table legs. The driver had apparently panicked when the bees began to escape and he just tossed it as hard as he could and got in his truck and left. We knew after we had discovered the transfer tube that the bees were somewhere close by.

Next he told him all about meeting Mr. Macy and about the problems that the bees had created around Grangeville with the two wolves and the lady's cat. Darrell told him how they had run an old mule to death and how they had attacked Desmond Macy's hunting dog and taken huge bites out of his hide. He then told him how the bees had swarmed on Mr. Macy's truck and how the beekeeper had become terrified of the aggressive bees and he was afraid to even go out to his hives.

My husband shook his head back and forth and said, "The poor beekeeper had not been back out to his hives until the night that we went out with him. He was just too afraid to go out there alone. It wasn't until we all went together during the evening that he discovered that they had all been destroyed by the wasps."

He continued on, "When we found all of his bees dead, Mr. Macy called other beekeepers around the valley and discovered their bees had all been killed by wasps too. The other beekeepers confirmed that the killer bees had not invaded any of their hives. All of their dead bees were just normal sized honeybees. Mr. Macy had the largest number of beehives in the area and his hives were the closest to the rest stop where the driver had let the bees escape."

My husband said, "We met several of the local beekeepers and we listened to them talk and they all decided that was probably the reason that the bees were drawn directly to Macy's hives. His hives were the most convenient."

My husband also added, "The night before we left, a lady from their newspaper and a man from a television station was there interviewing people and taking pictures. I think you need to be aware that by now the entire state knows about the giant bees, because Desmond Macy had them displayed on a table in the middle of the room so that everyone could see them. We never told anyone about the giant bees when we left Tower County, but the town of Grangeville is not keeping the killer bees confidential."

Dr. Keyes shook his head and responded, "There is nothing we can do to keep the giant bees a secret, besides we were only taking care of a problem that someone else had created. I don't care if everyone knows about the bees."

As he stared at the bee containers in amazement he said, "I can't believe that these terrifying monsters were taken down by wasps. I have been so disturbed about the bees ever since I talked with the truck driver that let them escape up near Grangeville." He again shook his head in disbelief as he handed the box and the pneumatic tube of bees back to my husband to keep. He said, "Well at least this atrocious heat-wave has been good for something. With all of the problems that it has created that is probably the only good thing that has come from this crazy phenomenon."

We watched as he stood up and kind of walked around in circles and then sat back down and put his face in his hands and rubbed his eyes. He shook his head back and forth again before talking, "I cannot believe that the problem with the killer bees is truly over. I could just imagine the havoc the bees could cause after they were established and they reproduced." He looked puzzled, "I am surprised that the giant bees would mix so easily with the smaller honeybees. It seems like with their massive size and their dominance they would chase the normal honeybees away and take over all of the beehives, but you said they were all together?"

My husband responded, "Yes, Mr. Macy told us that they were all in the beehives together from the very beginning and of course they were together when we found them after they had been killed by the wasps. It was almost as if they didn't realize that they were larger than the other bees."

TWENTY-EIGHT

The Real Problem

D r. Keyes then got out of his chair and kind of walked around in circles again and then walked over to where his wife was sitting in a bright yellow chair and put his hands on her shoulders as he told us, "I have to be honest with you, finding out that the bees are dead helps solve one of the problems that has really been disturbing me. Between the severe weather problems and the killer bees I have not been able to sleep for the past few weeks. I had no idea how honeybees dealt with the hot weather. I was so concerned that the bees would thrive in the heat and rapidly reproduce and then no one would be able to stop them."

He sighed before going on, "I saw how destructive they were when I was at the safety location in Tower County. I am so relieved to know that they are all dead; I can't begin to tell you how much better I feel knowing that they are really destroyed."

The doctor looked down at his beautiful wife and said, "If only the strange weather problems could be corrected that easily. We were originally sent here to Idaho to meet up with a group of research scientists that had been working on the radical changes taking place in the sun's rays, but they left before we got here."

He went on, "I had received several personal reports from the lead meteorologist of that group in the past few weeks. He had been telling me that his research team was getting threatening calls from their superiors. He told me to be cautious because their benefactors did not like the direction that the research was going in regards to bombings in the Middle East."

He sighed before going on, "The institutions that the scientists worked for knew that my team was meeting up with Dr. Rodgers' research team here in Lewiston and that tied our two research teams together. So, Dr. Rodgers told me to be cautious and to not use my regular cell phone, he said to only use a private secured number, so that's what I have been doing. Something really strange is going on here, very uncharacteristic of any other project that I have ever been involved in."

Dr. Keyes then sat down in his chair and put his face down into his hands, "I received a confidential fax shortly after I talked with you on the phone the other day, just as we were getting ready to leave Pennsylvania. It was a strange confusing letter, and it stated that the other group could no longer wait for us to arrive in Idaho. Dr. Rodgers said that his team felt that they were in danger, but I wasn't sure what they were talking about." Dr. Keyes looked up and said, "We almost didn't come, but I thought that they might change their minds and wait a few more hours when they realized that we were on our way." He looked over at his wife, "But they had already gone by the time we arrived."

He shrugged his shoulders and said, "They had been investigating the reasons for the shocking heat wave that was going on in several parts of the world. The research team along with my team had been sent to Idaho to help solve the severe weather and UV crisis and to help come up with a solution before it is too late. We were all sent to this area because of the sophisticated global weather system down here in the tunnel."

He shrugged his shoulders before going on, "We were supposed to get together to share our findings and come up with a solution to solve some of the problems causing the weird weather occurrences, but when we arrived we discovered that the other team truly was gone."

He wiped his hands over his face, "We are left here in Idaho to solve the situation by ourselves. In the fax that he sent me he told me that he had left all of his research documents locked up here in the vault at the safety location tunnel. When I checked the safe all of his documents were there just as he stated. Apparently, the research team silently slipped away only a few hours before we arrived."

The doctor shook his head, "We probably shouldn't have come to Idaho once I received the message, but the message made no sense to me." He wiped his hands across his face before going on, "We have known for a couple weeks that the research team had been threatened, but I didn't realize how serious the situation had become until we arrived and discovered that they were frightened enough to actually leave all of their documents behind."

Before going on, Dr. Keyes sent a security team to retrieve the research documents from the safe. When the security team arrived with the cart filled with the sealed documents he told us, "These are the notes that have been left for my team to go through. Their research team had accumulated 378 pages of documentation over the past few weeks, and they just left all of their reports behind in the safe." He shook his head in disbelief, "They must have been terribly frightened to sneak away and disregard all of their research."

He shrugged his shoulders and commented, "It is time to sift through all of their reports, because we have not been able to come up with any conclusive evidence by studying the weather screens. I have had technicians in several different parts of the earth continually following the weather monitors, but we have no conclusive evidence as to what is causing the heat-wave and violent UV rays. The situation is only growing worse and the severe weather is slowly destroying everything in its path."

He looked down at his wife again for reassurance before going on, "I brought my wife with me this time because the reports that we were getting in Pennsylvania were very disturbing." He covered his face with his hands and quickly wiped his eyes, "Friends, I am going to be honest with you, I brought my wife because I wanted us to stay together. Our kids do not live near us in Pennsylvania. Our daughter lives in Florida and our son is stationed in Germany."

He went on, "From all of the reports that have been coming in from around the world this is not a normal weather situation that we are dealing with. I did not want my wife Patty left alone in Pennsylvania with me 2000 miles away in Idaho, and unable to get back home."

He paused before going on, "The heat-wave is moving so quickly and it doesn't seem to be going away in any of the areas that it affects. He looked at his wife and then over at Dr. Tomlin who was now looking down towards the floor and he told us, "This odd weather situation is very alarming. I'm not sure that it can be stopped."

Staring down at his wife he muttered, "My greatest fear is that none of us will ever be able to leave this tunnel again, because our reports show that the areas that have been affected are remaining so hot that all of the crops are slowly dying and waterways are evaporating. It has gotten too hot in most areas to transport anything in trucks, vans and even the trains are being cancelled."

He looked over towards the window with the weather screens continually changing and he said, "We arrived on one of the last air flights that will be available until the heat-wave passes. The airport said that it is getting to hot in this area to fly planes in and out, even after dark."

He went on, "The strange weather has not reached Pennsylvania or anywhere nearby. We were still safe there. My people in Pennsylvania have been monitoring the disturbing weather situation ever since it first appeared in Canada, and we discovered that it has never cooled off in the areas that it impacts and the Ultra-Violet rays have never gotten any better."

He sighed, "Once it affects a region it never seems to go away. Some of the regions reported that the temperatures peaks at a certain high degree and then it does not go up any higher, but because the temperature never cools down everything is drying up. All of the rivers, crops, and food supply will soon be gone and the United States will be completely depended on other countries that are not affected."

Dr. Keyes looked ghostly white as he humbly told us, "I am so sorry that I ask you to risk so much to come and help us with the bees. Everything is worse than I could have ever imagined. When I called you several days ago, I had no idea that things would get this bad."

I looked at my husband and then quickly looked down at the floor; neither one of us knew what to say. All I could think about was, "We were so excited that we had taken care of the bees that we could hardly wait to show Dr. Keyes what we had found. Grangeville is so close to Lewiston and there was no reason for us not to come."

When I seriously thought about everything that had been going on in the past few days, I realized we probably wouldn't have done anything different even if we had known that there was a problem here at the safety location.

We have tried really hard to adjust to all of the strange events; we have learned to drive at night and we joked about wearing the weird sunglasses and the silly hats, and we were so focused on taking care of the killer bees that we never thought about the heat-wave problems being permanent and destroying all of the water and the food supply system. Suddenly everything is starting to become very real.

TWENTY-NINE

Dr. Samuel F. Rodgers

Dr. Keyes then told us, "The letter that I received a few minutes before I boarded the plane to come to Idaho was a faxed letter from Dr. Samuel F. Rodgers, the lead meteorologist with the United States Climatology Research Team. He was the person in charge that we were supposed to meet here in Lewiston. I had never met him, but I had talked with him on the phone several different times."

He continued, "Dr. Rodgers along with seven other scientists from around the world had been investigating the reasons for the shocking heat-wave that has recently inundated the northwestern part of the United States and is rapidly spreading throughout America."

He went on, "Their mission has taken them to all parts of the world. They started out their investigation trying to find accurate data on global warming, but after weeks of research they said that they found very few facts confirming the speculation theory of global warming, because everything was changing too rapidly. They knew that something immediate was causing all of the peculiar changes in the weather."

Dr. Keys then picked up the first stack of papers that were brought in from the safe. He stated, "Dr. Tomlin and I were just getting ready to unseal the files and start going through the endless piles of documentation. I do not feel comfortable sharing a lot of this classified information with the weather technicians that are working here at the tunnel, we do not even know them and we do not know who we can trust."

He said, "When we planned this mission we thought we would have the other research team here available to meet with us, and we would all work on the situation together. I only brought Dr. Tomlin and my wife with me this time, and there is no way that we can get through all of these papers by ourselves."

He looked over at Roberta Tomlin before saying, "Dr. Tomlin and I would welcome your help in sifting through the pages and pages of information if you are willing to help us. You have both worked with us before and you have proven to us that you can be trusted. I will be up front with you; this whole situation is too much for any of us to comprehend. I know that something is dreadfully wrong if the other scientists escaped early in the morning before dawn and left all of their documentation behind. They have been accumulating this information for a long time and a scientist will not just go off and leave their work in a safe for someone else to finish."

He gravely shook his head back and forth, "I do not know if we are all in danger or who the other team is even running from. I just hope that these stacks of documents will tell us what is going on once we read through them." He smiled at his wife and said, "Along with my wife Patty I'm sure the five of us should be able to read through the entire 378 pages of documents in no time. I noticed that many of notes are hand written and they are kind of hard to decipher, but if we each read a few pages at a time I think we can get through them."

The poor doctor looked exhausted, but he was determined to go on, "I am not sure what we will find in the piles of documents, but I fear from the message that Dr. Rodgers left me that we are going to discover some things that we really don't want to find out."

My husband looked over at me and kind of nodded his head and I nodded back so he told Dr. Keyes, "We can see that you really need some help, so we will be glad to help you sort through the papers."

Dr. Keyes smiled and then glanced down at his watch and he said, "It is almost 12:20, so let's order some lunch and take a break before we get started." Within a half an hour someone from the kitchen brought us each a small dinner salad, a variety of sandwiches, chips and a fresh fruit tray. On the cart was an ice bucket filled with individual juices, milk and water containers, but my husband was most thankful for the fresh thermos of coffee. He poured a cup of coffee, but he burned his lips as he impatiently tried to take a sip.

As we ate, my husband and I glanced at each other from across the table and kind of shook our heads. We had so many questions about the weather, the tunnel, the documents, and the strange statements that Dr. Keyes had said, but we could tell that the doctor was already under too much stress, so we decided to say nothing at this time. We quietly finished our lunch and decided to wait for a more appropriate time to talk about the prison that we had gotten ourselves into. Once again this entire situation seemed outrageous, but there was really nothing else that we could do but help our friends go through the documents.

By 3:00 in the afternoon, we were deep into the stacks of notes that had been put together by Dr. Rodgers and his research team. We discovered the names and information of Dr. Rodgers and each of the other doctors.

Dr. Samuel Rodgers, the lead Climatologist on the research team was a 53 year old Caucasian man from Salt Lake City, Utah with a wife and four grown children and seven grandchildren.

The second person on the team was **Dr. Peter Natanson**, a 61 year old Jewish man from Brooklyn, New York, who had recently lost his wife from cancer. He is a father of two married sons and he has four grandchildren.

The third person on the team is **Dr. Michael Renhur** from Kenya. He is a 46 year old African man with a wife and five children.

The fourth member of the team was **Dr. Mitchell Freed** from Sydney, Australia. He is a 49 year old Caucasian man with a wife and two college age daughters.

The fifth person on the team was **Dr. Kevin Smite** a 51 year old African-American man from Los Angeles, California. He has a wife and three children and two grandchildren.

The sixth person on the team was **Dr. William Zola** a 64 year old Hawaiian man from Honolulu, Hawaii. He was the oldest member of the team. He has a wife and three married children and six grandchildren.

The seventh member of the team was **Dr. James Ward** a 52 year old Caucasian man from Denver, Colorado with a wife and three grown children and no grandchildren.

The last person on the team was **Dr. David Trouse** a 37 year old Caucasian man from Boston, Massachusetts. He was single and the youngest member of the team.

As we gathered all of the pages, we found documentation from each one of the doctors. All of them had given a specific report on the things that they had researched. Each doctor played an important part in putting the source of the abnormal weather dilemma together.

We soon discovered how intelligent and honest the scientists really were. After reading just the first few pages we could tell why they were selected to be on this distinctive research team. They were each specialized in certain divisions of advanced climatology and as they worked together they complimented each other's expertise.

As we read through the reports we discovered that the eight man team had worked together on four other weather projects. The team was very compatible and their expertise had solved numerous unexplainable weather situations in various parts of the world.

One of the reasons that they worked so well as a team is because they could work individually at a project location and then get together as a group and bounce ideas and theories off of each other. This had proven to be very successful. We could tell by their notes that they listened and respected each other's opinion.

Reading through their notes, we were impressed by the scientists because they approached everything on a professional level. They worked only by scientific facts. Everything that they wrote about had to be proven, not estimated or guessed.

For the first few pages the information was light and upbeat. The doctors all seemed to get along really well; you could tell that they were good friends as well as colleagues. They truly enjoyed what they were doing. Each scientist documented that they felt that this assignment would be finished in around 10 day.

In the first documents they talked about places they visited while they were in Italy. All of the information was fun, friendly and brief. They seemed to have very little to say. All of the notes were short and to the point.

They had each traveled to Italy with the idea that the strange weather problems were caused by global warming and it could easily be proven. The institutions that they worked for had financed their venture to further prove the theory that our earth was being destroyed by global warming. That was their main objective for this weather research project.

The theory of Global Warming is a gradual increase in the overall temperature of the earth's atmosphere. It is generally attributed to the greenhouse effect caused by increased levels of carbon dioxide, chlorofluorocarbons and other pollutants that collects in the atmosphere. They feel that coal-burning power plants are one of the main causes for the carbon dioxide pollution. They believe that second largest cause is from so many automobiles.

From the beginning of their mission, the team was told that there was probably nothing they could do to solve the strange weather phenomenon. But they were encouraged to rapidly collect all of the data to prove that global warming was the cause of the change in weather before the weather conditions corrected themselves on their own.

On the first few pages, each doctor wrote that they were sure that within a few days they could prove to the world and to their financial foundations that the problems were all caused because of the global warming.

THIRTY

Questions

The research team was first sent to Italy because the air temperature had begun rising and the Ultra-violet sunrays were reported to be changing in Italy, France and Spain.

The sunrays in Italy were brighter than they normally were, but they were not unbearable like the UV rays were by the time they reached Canada and the United States.

One of the things that the scientists were to do was to interview the local residents and get their opinion on the changes that had occurred. They were told by the local people that they could tell that the sun's rays were different in Italy, but they didn't even need special glasses like the people did when the crisis came to America.

Immediately the research team went to work tracking the unusual atmospheric pressure changes. They could tell by their early readings that something was going on in the atmosphere that was changing the weather, but the reports were not clear as to the exact cause.

DAY THREE By their third day in Italy the scientists decided to do the day's research on their own. Each scientist was to track the strange weather patterns alone for the entire day and then meet up in the evening and compare their findings. This was the same way that the team had worked together on several different projects in the past. The scientists were experts and they normally came to the same professional conclusion with all of their data by the time they had finished and met up in the evening.

This project was different. When they met together at the end of the day they knew that something was really wrong because none of the facts that they put together added up. This had never happened to them before. Usually when they went their separate ways and monitored their own data they could get together at night and come up with a similar conclusion.

When we read through Dr. Rodgers notes from that day he wrote that the scientists were very concerned with the day's research. The research team had been there for three days and they were afraid that they were headed in the wrong direction. After three days of research notes, they were no closer to finding a reason for the unusual heat-wave than when they arrived.

He wrote that after cross-referencing all of the weather data they could tell the UV rays were changing because of the atmospheric air pressure not from the actual weather, but at that time none of the scientists could pinpoint where the changes in the atmospheric pressure were actually coming from.

DAY FOUR Dr. Smite wrote: After several days of hourly detailed statistics my research shows that the strange heat-wave is not caused by global warming. Dr. Smite was a renowned scientist from California who had produced years of data proving the global warming theory to be true. He was concerned with his research in Italy because none of the pieces fit together to specifically prove that the weather changes were caused by global warming. He was usually in the position to prove the global warming theory to be accurate, not inaccurate, so this was new to him.

Dr. Kevin Smite was a firm believer in global warming. He taught college classes on the subject, he had read over thirty books confirming the theory, and he had written extensive documents proving the theory to be true. He actively spoke at seminars preaching his theory because he firmly believed that the world would one day be destroyed because it was not being taken care of. He was an excellent instructor on global warming; that is why he was chosen for this team.

He was financially backed by several large contributors that believed in him and had sent him to Italy to support his research. They were certain that he could convince the rest of the team to find the problem to be caused by global warming and they would all arrive at the same conclusion rapidly. But Dr. Smite was also a brilliant meteorologist and he couldn't confirm something that he could not find conclusive statistics on.

DAY FIVE Dr. Mitchell Freed from Australia wrote: The weather changes in Italy are becoming quite a puzzle to each of us, because none of the facts go together. It appears that the changes in the atmospheric pressure actually came from someplace else. Their findings were inconclusive and totally different than they usually found. There was no definite solution for the changes in the temperature or the extreme Ultra-Violet sunrays.

DAY SIX Dr. Trouse from Boston wrote: Something is changing the atmospheric pressure and the sunshine is not being properly filtered like it is normally filtered. It is a problem that we have never dealt with before. He wrote: I know that something is upsetting the atmospheric pressure, but I am not clear just yet what is changing it.

*****

We sat in the office and read through piles and piles of information. We each took a small stack of papers and carefully read through every paragraph before discarding it or setting it in a special place. Many of the documents were of no importance and they added little value to the subject of the UV rays and the hot temperatures. We placed those papers in a dead file and no one would need to read through them again. When any of us came across any questionable weather information whatsoever we had Dr. Keyes and Dr. Tomlin read and study them and save them in a special box.

DAY SEVEN By the seventh day of their journey in Italy we noticed that the documents began to change. We could tell by the notes that the doctors wrote that they were becoming terribly discouraged. They were not finding the information that they were sent for and every one of the financial institutions that had sent the eight doctors was starting to complain. The project was extremely costly and the doctors were not sending the reports back that their supporters wanted to hear.

DAY EIGHT Dr. Zola from Honolulu, Hawaii wrote: Every night we are expected to contact our superiors from our own region or country, and tonight when I called I could tell that they are getting very upset with us. Today is the eighth day of our project, and none of our superiors are happy. They have invested a lot of money in this project and it is not going the way that they had planned. We have all been told to hurry up and prove the problem to be global warming and to wrap the project up. It is difficult for me to report something that I do not feel is accurate.

DAY TEN Dr. Samuel Rodgers wrote: Our superiors are threatening to send each of us home. It is day ten and we have still not figured out the true source of the change in the atmospheric pressure. We have all documented that we know that the atmospheric pressure is what is causing the problem, but after several intense days of research our findings are still inconclusive.

DAY FOURTEEN Dr. Peter Natanson from Brooklyn, New York wrote: We have been traveling throughout Italy for the past two weeks and we are all getting very discouraged because the unsettling weather does not make any sense to us. I have been talking it over with my colleagues and we feel that we are looking in the wrong direction. Dr. Renhur and I have been trying to convince the rest of the team to fly to Israel and not go on to France at this time, because all of our statistics of the unfiltered UV rays are being tracked in the atmosphere from that direction. Our reports are inconclusive, but we are beginning to suspect that something is interfering with the atmospheric pressure and that is what is changing the UV rays. The unsafe ultra-violet sunrays are the main problem that we are dealing with. It is far more dangerous than the hot weather. The effects on the atmospheric pressure are similar to global warming, but they are not gradual like global warming, they are happening much faster; almost instantaneously.

DAY SIXTEEN Dr. James Ward wrote: We are starting to get threats from our supervisors. Against our administrators wishes, our team boarded a plane to fly into Israel to see if we can get to the root of this strange weather problem. We were sent here on a mission and we want to get to the core of this situation before we go back to our homes.

THIRTY-ONE

Israel

D r. Rodgers wrote: We arrived in Israel early this morning. Israel is continually under attack. There is a rocket fired on Israel every six minutes twenty-four hours a day. The only reason that Israel has survived all of the bombings is because of its defense system called the Iron Dome. The extraordinary defense system blows the rockets into pieces before the rocket can hit the target. The Israeli officials claimed that the system has intercepted up to 85 per cent of the rockets fired from Gaza. My team is puzzled because the heat-wave and unfiltered UV rays have not affected Israel even with all of the bombings going on.

As we each study our own personal weather data we document that the unusual weather patterns are beyond Israel off towards Italy. Later, as we talked about the continual bombings that take place every few minutes Dr. Freed asked me the question, "Where do all of the particles go that are blown apart by the Iron Dome Defense System?"

DAY NINETEEN Dr. Samuel Rodgers wrote: My team has been in Israel for three days and all of our data conclusively confirms the changes in the atmospheric pressure are caused by the billions of minute particles that have been blown apart in the atmosphere by the Iron Dome Defense System. After months of continual bombings we feel that the atmosphere can no longer filter out the sun's harmful sunrays.

We have sent this information to all of our superiors, but they refuse to accept this as the problem. We are surprised at their response. They demand that we return to Italy immediately and to not share our findings with anyone. For the first time in our research history, my team is afraid. With all of the wars and violence taking place in every part of the world we can no longer tell our friends from our enemies. Even our own administrators have turned on us. Every one of us feels all alone.

EVENING OF DAY NINETEEN Dr. Kevin Smite, the Professor of Global Warming from Los Angeles, California wrote: We will leave Israel tomorrow morning and return to Italy as our advisors demanded, but I have posted all of my documentation in my blog for other scientists to read. This situation is very critical, the continual bombings have got to cease or we will eventually destroy the world's atmospheric pressure.

DAY TWENTY Dr. Samuel Rodgers, the lead Climatologists for the research team wrote: Our team has returned to Italy just as our advisors demanded that we do, but they are insisting that we document our findings as global warming and we all know that that is not the truth. For some reason they do not want to admit that the bombings are causing atmospheric changes around the world.

He wrote: We had a little difficulty early this morning when we left our rooms and went down to the rental van to prepare to move on to Spain. We discovered that all four tires had been sliced and destroyed. The tires were unusable and we were forced to wait a good portion of the day for new tires to arrive so that we could move on into Spain.

THAT EVENING Dr. Rodgers wrote: It had taken us all day to get the tires replaced so we were forced to stay in Italy for another night. I would have thought that the sliced tires were just a random act of violence, but at dinner this evening I received a sealed letter at our table warning me to **'withdraw'**. The letter was delivered on a silver plate by one of the waiters, so none of us saw where the letter had come from. Even after diligently looking around the restaurant we saw no one that we recognized.

LATER THAT EVENING in the hotel room Dr. James Ward wrote: We all call home every night to make sure that our families know where we are staying and that we are alright. I was disturbed when I called home tonight because someone had vandalized my house while my wife was gone to church. They had spray painted orange paint all across our back deck. My wife was really scared because the person had been brave enough to come in our backyard, during the daytime to destroy our property. We live in a very safe neighborhood and incidents like this never happen. She had called the police and they had interviewed many of the close neighbors, but not one person had seen anything. I asked my brother to stay at the house until I can get back home.

THIRTY-TWO

Time to Rest

We had been reading through the stacks of papers all day long and we were all getting really tired. It was 4:23 in the afternoon and Darrell and I could hardly stay awake because we hadn't slept since yesterday afternoon in our motel room. We had the party with the people in Grangeville yesterday evening and then we drove all night to get here. So we had been up all night and all day.

Dr. Keyes called for someone to come and find us a room to rest for a few hours. He decided that this was a good time to stop. The documents that we had been reading through were starting to get very intense.

Dr. Keyes locked all of the documents inside the office and he and his wife exhaustedly went off to their room. Dr. Tomlin went to her room and we followed a young soldier down the hall to a place for us to stay.

Our room was not very far away from the office where we had been working. It was decided before we left that we would meet in three hours to have dinner and get started sorting through the documents again.

The rooms in this safety location were more like those in an Army barracks. They were much smaller than the rooms in Tower County and they were located directly off of the tunnel. Each door was metal and this time they could lock. The small room was all white with a sink, mirror and one chair. The nice thing about this room was that it had its own private bathroom and shower off to the corner of the sink. It had a tiny free-standing closet with two military style bunk beds up against one wall. The beds had very firm mattresses with one pillow, crisp white sheets and one folded blanket at the end of the cot. There were no windows so it was difficult to tell exactly what time it was. But we climbed into bed and within seconds we were both asleep.

Three hours later we heard a knock on the door letting us know that it was 7:20 and dinner would be ready in ten minutes.

After quickly cleaning up for dinner, we unlocked the door and headed towards the office. When we reached the office, we stopped short in our tracks, because the office door that had been locked when we left was now slightly ajar and we feared someone had gotten into to the private files.

As we crept up slowly to the door we could see Dr. Keyes and his wife Patty down the hallway walking towards us. When he approached the office my husband whispered, "Someone has been into the office, because I saw you lock the door when we left, and it is no longer locked."

The four of us cautiously walked up to the door and decided to quickly push it open. As the door flung opened we saw Dr. Tomlin sitting behind the desk solemnly reading through a pile of documents with only one small lit desk lamp glowing. She looked up from her papers as the four of us dauntingly leaped through the door.

"You about frightened me to death," she screamed. "Why did you all come through the door at once?"

We couldn't help it. All four of us broke out laughing. We must have looked like quite a menacing group; all of us jumping through the doorway at one time. Dr. Keyes finally stopped laughing and apologized.

He told her, "I'm sorry, I guess we are all kind of edgy after everything that has been going on with the strange weather and the things that we have been reading. We were afraid that someone had gotten into the office."

She smiled and said, "I couldn't rest so I came back down to the office and used my key to get back in and started reading again. I didn't want to disturb anyone so I didn't turn all of the lights on. I have been down here for over two hours. I have already finished two whole cups of coffee." She shook her head back and forth and got really serious, "You are not going to believe some of the things that I have come across." She picked up the last paper that she had read and showed it to Dr. Keyes and then got up and walked around the room shaking her head.

After Dr. Keyes read the paper he said, "No wonder the doctors were so afraid. What is going on here?" Before Dr. Tomlin could respond a man came in the office pushing a cart with our dinner on it.

Patty Keyes placed the plates full of food and silverware on the clean table cloth on the table in the back of the room and I put a water glass and a cup at the side of each place. On the bottom shelf of the cart was a pitcher of water, orange juice, and a thermos of hot water for tea, and one for coffee. I poured coffee, water, juice and hot tea for anyone who needed them.

Our dinner looked delicious, they had prepared pork chops, potatoes and gravy and fresh asparagus. We had a small bowl of applesauce on each plate and a tray filled with fresh baked rolls and butter. The kitchen had also brought each of us a freshly baked piece of cherry pie with a dollop of whipped cream on each slice.

We could tell that Dr. Keyes had to force himself to eat after reading the disturbing paper. It was a good thing that his wife Patty was here with him because she forced him to eat and she wouldn't let him give in. She told him, "We have a long night ahead of us and you need all of the fuel that you can get."

He shook his head up and down and smiled at her and graciously ate most of his dinner. They were such a good looking couple and they seemed to get along really well. She was very convincing, because he even ate a good portion of his pie.

When everyone was finished with the delicious dinner and had their coffee or hot tea we decided it was time to get started again. We had a lot of reading ahead of us.

THIRTY-THREE

The Documents

We each looked over several of the papers that Dr. Tomlin had read earlier. She wanted to bring us up to where we had left off at 4:20.

DAY TWENTY-ONE Dr. Kevin Smite from Los Angeles, California wrote: I am getting a lot of pressure from my benefactors to tie up this unusual research project. They demand that I document the project as global warming. They want me to come home. They are very angry about what I wrote in my blog when I was in Israel. When I refused to change my reports, they threatened me by saying they would cut off all of my funding if I didn't do what they wanted. I am afraid if my funding is dropped I will no longer have my job, but I refuse to lie about what is causing the strange weather problems. I'm not sure what to do.

THAT EVENING Dr. Kevin Smite wrote: I have talked it over with my wife and she wants me to come home. She found a note on her car window this morning when she was at the grocery store. It was a letter inside of a sealed envelope and the letter said: **"Convince your husband or your family will be sorry."**

DAY TWENTY-TWO Dr. Samuel Rodgers wrote: We heard on the National Weather News reports that the disturbing weather changes have now reached across Canada and down through Montana, Northern Idaho, Washington, Oregon, California, Nevada and Southwest Idaho. This is very frightening news for us because we have been notified that it is much more severe in the states than it was when it first started in Italy. We have been told that the weather is much hotter in Canada and in the states that have been affected and the Ultra-Violet rays are getting worse as they rapidly move across America.

EVENING OF DAY TWENTY-TWO Dr. Peter Natanson of Brooklyn, New York wrote that both of his sons received threatening letters in the mail today. The most frightening thing about the threats is that one son lives in Brooklyn, but the other son lives in Texas.

DAY TWENTY-THREE Dr. Michael Renhur of Kenya, South Africa wrote: Some men went to my house yesterday and frightened my wife and 5 children so much that my wife begged me to tell everyone whatever my superiors wanted me to say. I am shocked by my wife's response because she is very honest and very brave, but she sounded so terrified I didn't know what to tell her. My wife is pregnant with our 6th child and I am so far away that I can not protect my family.

ALSO DAY TWENTY-THREE Dr. Michael Freed from Sidney, Australia wrote I must go home. My two daughters were each approached by two American men in dark suits yesterday. One of my daughters is at the local college, but the other one is in college in France.

ALSO ON DAY TWENTY-THREE Dr. David Trouse from Boston, Massachusetts wrote: I got a message from my father this morning stating that my mother had been abducted. I have been worried sick all day. I just received word that she was found unharmed. Her abductors left her at a park 100 miles away from my parent's house.

ALSO ON DAY TWENTY-THREE Dr. William Zola from Honolulu, Hawaii wrote: My 10 year old granddaughter called me this morning and begged me to come home. She told me that someone keeps calling Grandma's cell phone number and hanging up. They have called her two times an hour, day and night for the past three days. Aleesha, my granddaughter told me that her Grandma is so afraid that she will no longer answer her phone.

Darrell leaned over and whispered in my ear, "Remember when Dr. Keyes first called us on my cell phone at the restaurant and wanted us to call him back. When we called him back he wouldn't answer and we found out later he was afraid that his phone was bugged. Then someone kept calling my cell phone several times a day and hanging up. He must have been right. They had bugged his phone. Because they were doing the same thing to me that they are doing to Dr. Zola's wife."

ALSO ON DAY TWENTY-THREE Dr. Samuel Rodgers the lead Climatologist wrote: I am so shocked and disappointed at the things that I have witnessed. We were sent here to help with a severe weather phenomenon and now we must all fear for our lives. Our superiors have threatened each one of us. When that did not work they threatened our jobs, and now they have threatened our families. I can not believe all of this.

We are scientists; we are not criminals, killers or terrorist. We are professional Climatologists who are trained to track down strange weather problems. How did this project get so far off course? It is all about the money. There is so much greed involved in proving who is right and who is wrong that it has put every one of our lives in danger.

The most frightening thing about this whole situation is that they seem to be stalking our families. They always know where they are and what they are doing. At church, at the grocery store, at their schools, at their work sites even if parts of our families are in different states or different countries; they have also visited them. We feel absolutely helpless because we are thousands of miles away from our homes and there is no way any one of us can protect our loved ones. When will this foolishness stop?

This is bizarre; we have never felt we have needed to protect our families before while we are away working on a weather project.

Our entire world has gone crazy. I watch the news and I am so surprised at the hatred for the Christians, Muslims, illegal immigrants, people in authority, the military, firemen, policemen and now Climatologists. When will it come to an end? All we see is hatred and greed and there is no value for human life. To me the most important thing in the world is my wife and my family.

Tomorrow we leave Italy and we will fly across the Atlantic Ocean, over Canada and all the way to Lewiston, Idaho. It will take us 36 hours to get there, but that is the place where the global weather laboratory is located. It is the key weather center of the world. From the core of a mountain we can track the weather anywhere throughout the globe. We will meet up with a team of specialists from Pennsylvania and together we can decide what we need to do about the heat-wave and the abnormal UV rays.

DAY TWENTY-FOUR Dr. Samuel Rodgers wrote: When we got ready to leave the hotel this morning we discovered that Dr. Mitchell Freed had boarded a red-eye flight late last night and flew home to Australia. He left a note on his nightstand asking all of us to forgive him for leaving, but he was worried about his wife and his two college age daughters.

ALSO DAY TWENTY-FOUR Dr. Samuel Rodgers wrote: We also found a note from Dr. Michael Renhur from Kenya. He wrote, I am sorry to let the team down, but I must return home, I must protect my family.

EVENING OF DAY TWENTY-FIVE DR. Samuel Rodgers wrote: We arrived in Lewiston around 9:30 this evening. The trip went uneventful. Most of us slept through the whole flight. We have been in and out of a plane for the past 36 hours and we are glad to finally be on solid ground.

The temperature in Lewiston, Idaho is unreal. When we got off of the plane it was 118 degrees. It is already dark out, but the weather does not seem to be cooling down. We were picked up at the airport by a military escort and taken to an odd safety location high up on top of a hill above Lewiston. When we reached the top of the mountain we soon discovered that we had arrived at the famed Lewiston Hill global weather laboratory, the key weather center of the world.

Traveling to the core of the mountain was an extraordinary experience. It is so completely different than anywhere else on this earth that we have ever been. It is an exceptional facility. What a unique idea to build a tunnel to move an entire military unit and also house the world's safest weather location. We were all in awe of the tunnel's operation.

DAY TWENTY-SIX Dr. Samuel Rodgers wrote: Luckily, we can still receive text messages on our phones inside of the mountain. I am quite surprised, but pleased that I can hear from home. Every one of the scientist have tried to reach their families to check on them.

DAY TWENTY-SIX Dr. William Zola wrote: My son turned off my wife's phone and promised that he would stay at the house with his mother until I return home.

A few hours later I received a call from my son. He told me that there had been a black car sitting in the driveway for the past several hours. I told my son to call the police. When I called him back a few minutes later the phone just rang and rang, but nobody answered. I am really worried.

DAY TWENTY-SIX Dr. David Trouse wrote: I was unable to reach my parents tonight, and I have tried several different times. The last report that I had received said that my mother was safely home with my father, but I don't understand why they won't answer the phone.

DAY TWENTY-SIX Dr. Peter Natanson wrote: I called both of my sons, but their phones just rang and rang no one ever answered.

DAY TWENTY-SIX Dr. Kevin Smite wrote: I refuse to try to call home. I am disappointed at the severe reaction that my superiors have had towards my research documentation on Israel. I cannot believe that they have turned on me so quickly. Of course I still firmly believe in the theory of global warming. I have spent my entire adult life trying to convince others of my belief, but I will not be bullied. I am very determined, perhaps even stubborn and I am not going to be forced to report something I know is incorrect.

We were almost finished reading all of the documents. We had placed the ones that we couldn't understand in a certain bin for Dr. Keyes or Dr. Tomlin to look over. Some of the weather terminology was too difficult for us to read, and we knew that they would recognize what was actually happening in the reports in regards to the heat-wave and the dangerous UV rays. The two doctors had already read through all of those reports too. Patty, Darrell and I had finished reading the general documents and we had stacked them in piles of importance. When we got to the last of the papers in the pile Dr. Tomlin pulled out the paper that she had read hours earlier when she had been scanning through all of the papers before we had dinner. She first handed the troubling document to Dr. Keyes and he handed it to my husband to read.

DAY TWENTY-SEVEN Dr. Samuel Rodgers wrote: I feel like I am making this up, because the whole situation is so unreal. It is so far beyond my comprehension, yet I know that it is really happening. Even when I stop and go back over the past several days I cannot remember how I got here. How did I get to this point of no return? I have never lived dangerously or taken any careless risk, so how did I get to this place of hopelessness?

An hour ago my wife faxed me a newspaper article that she had received at her office. She said that it had arrived in a special marked envelope that read: personal "for your eyes only." When she opened the sealed envelope, she almost fainted. It was a fake copy of my obituary that looked like it had been taken out of the newspaper. It had my picture on the top of the article and it was dated three days from now.

It is not yet daylight, so we can still take a plane out of Lewiston this morning. My team and I are preparing to leave within the hour. We have requested a military vehicle to return us to the airport. We are so sorry, but we cannot wait any longer. We must get to our homes and try to straighten out the difficulties that have been created. It is not just our lives that are involved in this problem; it is the lives of everyone that we love.

We have not changed our minds on what has caused the bizarre weather phenomenon. We know that the problem that is causing the unusual heat-wave and the blinding ultra-violet sunrays starts with the bombings of Israel. There have always been wars and rumors of wars, but finally our atmosphere can take no more and it is striking back. The only solution to this problem is for the bombings to stop. I am sure if the bombings were to cease our world would slowly return to the way that it was before the atmosphere became so cluttered. We have made copies of our most vital research documents and we will take them with us as evidence.

I have already faxed you a letter explaining our immediate departure. Sorry we weren't at the safety location to meet with you when you arrived. I looked forward to cross-referencing ideas with you. I hope we can meet up another time under better circumstances. After twenty-seven days of research my team has arrived at the only reasonable conclusion possible; because we went right to the source of the problem and observed the problem with our own eyes. Our minds cannot be changed; the problems causing the astonishing heat-wave and unbearable Ultra-Violet sunrays begin with the bombings in Israel.

Good luck to all of you and may God keep you safe,

Dr. Samuel F. Rodgers

United States Climatology Research Team

THIRTY-FOUR

Now What

It was 4:00 in the morning when we had finished reading every one of the documents left behind by the research team. All of our minds were on over-load. So much had happened in the past twenty-four hours. The research team that we had followed so diligently was most likely home by now. I only prayed that their lives could get back to some kind of normal.

It was hard for all of us to grasp everything that we had read. Sorting through 378 pages of heavy informational documents is incredible, but between all five of us we did it. We didn't stop until we had covered all of the documents in the files. Once we finished every page our minds could not calm down, but around 4:30 we decided to head to our rooms and try to get some sleep.

At 10:00 a.m. the next morning one of the technicians knocked on our door and told us to come see what was being reported on the television monitors. We bolted down the hall and as we sat down to watch one of the wide screen televisions, we were surprised to see a nice looking middle-aged man by the name of Dr. Samuel Rodgers of Salt Lake City,

Utah speaking on National television. The heading on the news report was titled **'Special Report'** from the White House.

Dr. Rodgers began the report by sharing his thoughts about the continual bombings in Israel. He said, "After multiple days of researching the unusual weather phenomenon and the troubling UV rays my team of experts have concluded that the problems are the result of a type of global warming caused by the multiple bombings taking place in the Middle East."

He stated, "There is a bomb intercepted by the Iron Dome Defense system in Israel every six minutes, twenty-four hours a day. My team has determined that the exploded particles are going out into our atmosphere and causing the atmospheric pressure to drastically change until the UV rays will no longer filter out the sun's dangerous rays."

Dr. Rodgers looked directly into the camera and stated, "Unless the bombings cease our entire world as we know it will no longer survive. There have always been wars and rumors of wars, but the atmosphere is finally striking back and it can take no more. If we continue to destroy the atmosphere the Ultra-violet sunrays will persistently get worse and soon they will no longer be able to filter out the dangerous rays and everything throughout the earth will burn up. The only difference in this report and the theory of global warming is that this is happening **NOW**. It is not gradual and it will not be 100 or 200 hundred years away. It might be in two weeks or next month. It has already traveled across Italy, France, Spain, Canada and half way across America. We are watching this destruction happen right before our own eyes."

After Dr. Rodgers finished, we all just sat silently in our chairs and continued to stair at the television. We were stunned. After a few seconds Dr. Keyes muttered, "The man is brilliant."

Three hours later a giant caption scrolled across the wide screens: **ALL BOMBINGS HAVE CEASED THROUGHOUT THE WORLD.**

The entire room broke out in cheers. Dr. Keys smiled, "He did it. I'm not sure how long it will last, but he did it. He got the world to pay attention." He went on, "People are not concerned about what might happen in a hundred years, but everyone around the globe can relate to now, because that affects them."

That afternoon I called each of our kids and told them that we loved them and we would be home in a few days. Grandpa talked to them too and he told them that we had just about finished up the work that we were doing for our friend. It was so great to hear their voices and to know that things would soon be back to the way they were. As my husband talked to each of our kids, I quickly turned my head to wipe away the tears that were running down my face.

As I looked up I saw Patty Keyes standing only a few feet away watching me. She quickly held out her arms and we stood together crying and hugging each other, because this nightmare was almost over and we both will get to go home.

By the next morning, weather reports from all around the country were changing. The temperatures were already starting to drop. Within a day they were dropping by as much as 1 degree every 12 hours and the ultra-violet rays were slipping back into the safety zone. Our world will soon be back to normal and we will all be able to leave the safety location.

Within five days the weather had cooled off enough outside for us to safely leave the tunnel. The planes were flying again and Dr. Keyes, his wife Patty and Dr. Tomlin could head back to Pennsylvania knowing that they had helped save the world.

We had all become good friends. Together we had fought the winds of Tower County, the giant killer bees, the horrendous heat-wave and the lethal UV sunrays. I smiled, "We will be friends for life."

With both sadness and joy we said our goodbyes to everyone and climbed into the military Jeep to go back to get our vehicle. We were driven back to our car by the same nice young soldier that we met when we had first arrived at the safety location. As we headed out of the tunnel I realized the young man had been right, it isn't scary after you've been in here for a few days. You do feel right at home.

I glanced down at the box of bees that we were taking home; most where in pieces and some were the whole bees that we had gotten out of the transfer tube. I was excited because, I would have something to show my grandkids.

As we drove out of the tunnel and into the bright sunlight we once again put on our strange looking sunglasses...just to be safe. The UV rays were not quite as glaring as they had been when we first left Boise, but they were still not completely back to normal. Our eyes also needed time to adjust because we had been living underground in a tunnel for several days.

When we came out of the safety location we drove the rest of the way up the Old Spiral Highway to where it connects with the new highway. As we pulled out onto the thoroughfare and headed down the steep Lewiston Hill grade it almost took my breath away. To think that we were driving over the top of the secret military tunnel, the safety location and the famous Global Weather Laboratory, the key weather center of the world.

It was inconceivable because we had been staying inside of this mountain, 1,500 hundred feet underground. There is so much more substance to the towering Lewiston Hill grade than anyone could ever imagine. It will never just be a wide high-speed highway to me again. It is an unbelievable accolade for Idaho; just one more secret for us to never share with anyone.

I rolled down the window and let the hot breeze blow through my hair. Life is good. The last few days have been absolutely incredible. One can never even guess how an absolutely hopeless situation can instantly change. Sometimes you just need to hang on and wait until tomorrow.

The weather had dropped several degrees since we first arrived. It was a comfortable 103 degrees, a perfect day for a drive home. When we had first come to Grangeville and Lewiston last week we drove in through Ontario, Weiser, New Meadows and Riggins, before going on to Grangeville and Lewiston. With the confusing weather we were forced to travel during the middle of the night. But today we can be out in the sunlight. Today is a new day and we can drive home during the daytime and not be afraid. Since we came in on Highway 95 we thought it would be nice to go home through Long Valley.

THIRTY-FIVE

Long Valley

State Highway 55 is called the Payette River Scenic Byway; it is a designated National scenic byway and it is the main north-south route through Long Valley.

Long Valley extends over 30 miles from Payette Lakes at McCall to the south of Cascade at Round Valley. Valley County, named after the Long Valley, was established in 1917. Long Valley was formerly a summer pasture for livestock for the ranchers from the Boise Valley. By 1889 the ranchers from the Boise Valley would bring large herds up to Long Valley and it would upset the homesteaders living there.

The homesteaders would get angry and try to stop the ranchers in Boise Valley from using what they felt was their land, but when the ranchers wouldn't stop, the homesteaders retaliated by slaughtering all of the cattle.

Since the completion of the Cascade Dam in 1948 much of the northern part of the valley has been covered by the Cascade Reservoir and many of the original homesteads had to be relocated.

Prior to the Idaho gold rush of the 1860's, Native Americans camped in Round Valley to hunt and dig dry camas roots. Packer John Welch contracted freight supplies from Umatilla Landing on the Columbia River all the way up to Idaho City. He established a brush camp on the clear creek in 1860 which became Cascade.

In 1886 Jack Jasper and a man named J.W. Pottenger established the little town of Roseberry.

Roseberry is nestled in Long Valley within the Rocky Mountains. In 1911 it was the largest town in the valley. The railroad came through in 1914 and the Union Pacific completed its track from Emmett to McCall making the logging business profitable. All of the little towns that were not directly on the railroad died off leaving Roseberry a ghost town. The Roseberry store stood empty until 1950 when it was used as a honey house where they canned and sold honey.

My thoughts were interrupted when I noticed we had passed the town of Cottonwood where the beehives were located, and we would soon be back to Grangeville. I smiled as I thought about our friends Mr. Macy, the mayor, the two policemen and Bill and Lisa Riley.

As we drove by the truck stop where we had spent so many hours talking with our new friends, I was pleased to see that the business was once again filled with people. I casually glanced down the road that led into the center of town and I realized that we will never see Grangeville the same way again. We have such a bond with these people because of the giant bees, and that bond can never be broken.

Within a few minutes we had reached the top of the abrupt White Bird Summit and we started down the steep incline. Slowly passing the rest area where we had discovered the first of the giant bees. I shivered when I remembered the pure terror that I felt standing out there in the darkness wondering where the killer bees could be. I remember being frightened to death that we might find them, yet equally scared that we might not. There was no reason for us to stop again; our job here was done.

I couldn't help but beam as I viewed the elegant mountain range. I was in awe of the surroundings and I told my husband, "The Mountains are so beautiful this time of the year; and after all that has happened in the past few days they look pristine even seeing them through our strange sunglasses." I smiled and said, "I am so thankful because the world is at peace for the first time in my lifetime. The bible says it will not last, but at least for today there is peace."

In less than an hour we got back to New Meadows. New Meadows hosts the last surviving Pacific and Idaho Northern Railroad Depot. Without the railroad New Meadows would not have existed. The depot was built in 1910 and New Meadows was founded in 1911. It is listed on the National Register of Historical Places.

When we came to the stop sign at the junction in New Meadows, we turned to the left and headed towards McCall on Idaho 55. This is the beginning of the Payette River Scenic Byway. The settlement of McCall was established by Thomas and Louisa McCall in 1889. McCall held squatters rights to a cabin and 160 acres; the cabin was located near the present day Hotel McCall.

We soon arrived in McCall and found a place to park next to the curb, right in the center of town. It was time for a coffee break. It was incredible seeing all of the people walking around. We had all remained hidden inside of our houses and businesses for the past several weeks, and now we are free. We can be outside in the daytime and it feels wonderful. The town is surrounded by forests and it is always quite a bit cooler in McCall. As we walked past the corner store we saw an exterior temperature gauge and it read 99 degrees. Halleluiah! Our world is getting back to normal.

We leisurely drank our coffee and the two of us shared a warm scone and then went back to the car to head to Boise. We left McCall, and headed to Donnelly and Cascade and drove straight through the town of Horseshoe Bend without stopping. We would soon be home.

We pulled into our driveway around 3:00 in the afternoon. The temperature was a pleasing 99 degrees. It had always remained cooler here in Boise than it had been in Lewiston, but 99 seemed perfect to me.

When I walked in the house my mind was on over-load. I sat down for a few minutes and just kind of stared into space. So many weird things had happened and I had several things that I needed to do, but I couldn't seem to sort everything out.

Darrell went outside to mow the lawn because it hadn't been mowed in over two weeks and with the severely hot weather is was very dry. He wanted to mow it and get it watered.

While he was still mowing the lawn, I walked across the street to say hello to our neighbor Arlene. She had picked up the few pieces of mail that had been delivered while we were away, and we chatted for a couple of minutes and then I headed back home.

I could hear the mower going in the backyard, so I went to the phone and made several quick calls just to let people know that we had gotten home safely. I called Margaret, my sister Suzanne, Connie, Carolyn, and Darlene. I had to leave messages on several of the answering machines because most of them were not home. I then called all of our kids to tell them that we had made it home safely.

I couldn't wait to show the grandkids the bees, so we made plans for them to come over later this evening. I told them I had a surprise to show them, but I wouldn't tell them what it was.

Everyone that I talked to on the phone was so glad to have the heat-wave pass, but no one was more delighted than me. I was home and for a few scary days I wasn't sure if I would ever be able to come home again.

I looked around the room and realized that I needed to straighten things up before all of the kids came over, but I had a hard time getting started. I had so many thoughts floating around inside of my head.

Finally, after making a couple of salads and organizing things for dinner, I headed for the shower. I was tired and ready to get cleaned up.

Before getting in the shower I went to my dresser drawer to get a few things out to wear and I discovered that a full bottle of lotion had come open and spilled throughout the entire top drawer, and it drenched everything in its path. It must have gotten too hot while we were gone to Lewiston. The lotion had completely emptied all over the drawer. It was a sticky mess.

I got a plastic tub out of the garage and started plopping all of the sloppy items into the tub so that I could take care of them later. After everything was removed from the drawer, I noticed a picture stuck upside down under the gooey lotion. As I picked up the destroyed photo, I realized it was my cherished picture of my friends and me as we sat high up on a mountaintop watching the raging fire below us. It was the picture that someone had mysteriously sent to me in a card when we first returned from Tower County. It was the only thing that I had left from our journey with our friends as we were searching for the light, but now it was gone too.

Even as I stared at the destroyed photo, the faces began to fade and blur right before my eyes until the entire picture was completely white and no longer distinguishable. For one second, my heart felt sad at the loss of the treasured photograph. But I had looked at the picture so many times since I received it, that the image was engraved in the depths of my heart and my mind.

Without shedding any tears over my lost photo. I dumped the soggy picture in the tub along with the other items and decided it was time to get ready for my family, they would be here soon.

THIRTY-SIX

Let Me Explain

At around 7:00 p.m. that evening our entire family started to arrive. By 7:30 all fifteen of us, plus Marissa, Michael's girlfriend sat down out on the deck for hamburgers, chips, salads and homemade lemonade. Hailie and Darrek were both home from college and that made the family complete.

The heat-wave has caused so much disorder in everyone's life, that people were ready to get outside again and enjoy the rest of the summer. They were basking in the nice weather conditions trying to make up for the days that they had lost. The news reports stated that the UV rays were now at a safe level, and people could go outside without wearing the strange sunglasses.

When dinner was finished, our grandson Darrek asked us about our trip and brought up a story that he had seen on television. He told us, "They showed pictures of some giant killer bees that had been found up near Grangeville." He said, "We were all really worried about you because we knew that was the area where you were going. We are glad that you got to go help your friend and all, but we couldn't believe that you were up there with the giant African killer bees around. Can you imagine if you would have seen them?"

Hailie laughingly joined in, "Well of course they probably couldn't have really seen them. The television said that no one would go out during the daytime because it was too hot, and bees don't go out at night."

Our son Darren added, "Oh, I know, they said that it was even hotter up there than it was here; the television said it was like 117 degrees during the daytime" He laughed as he held out both hands and shrugged his shoulders "It never got above 113 in Boise."

That got the conversation going and our daughter Debi said, "Oh, I hate bees, and those bees were so huge. I can't imagine seeing one of those in my backyard."

Sammy our daughter-in-law laughed as she added, "Can you believe the honey those things would produce? They said that each one of the giant bees is about two inches long and about a half an inch across. They are almost as big as humming birds."

Our youngest daughter Dani shook her head back and forth as she eagerly stated, "I know that is crazy! How could bees ever get that big?"

Even our quiet grandson Devon spoke up doing his Morgan Freeman impersonation, "I think they would be cool to see. I would love to see one." He chuckled, "I would want them to already be dead of course."

I looked over at Grandpa and motioned for him to go and get the bees.

As he brought them out to the deck in the box I cautiously told our family, "Well we told you we had a surprise for you." As we opened the box of giant bees everybody gasped.

Our oldest grandson Michael shouted, "Where did you get these? You just can't bring home someone's giant bees that are lying around."

I couldn't help but laugh, "We didn't just bring them home, that's why we went to Grangeville in the first place, to find the giant killer bees for our friend. He called us and told us that a truck driver had let them escape in a rest area up near Grangeville and he didn't have anyone else to go find them. That's why we left in the middle of the night even with a heat-wave going on; because he needed our help."

Every one of our kids and grandkids just stood there with their mouths open and stared at the two of us. No one said a word.

Darrell and I couldn't help it, they looked so shocked. We finally just burst out laughing at the way they were looking at us, but none of them were laughing. They just stood there and stared at us. They acted like we had both grown two heads.

My husband broke the silence by explaining how we had become good friends with Dr. David Benjamin Keyes the lead meteorologist from Pennsylvania. He told the family, "We met him when we were in Pocatello finding Suzanne and Gene and we had worked with him on another project." He went on, "The doctor needed someone who knew about the bees to go and find them after they were let loose up near Grangeville; so that is why he called us."

But that explanation didn't seem to help either, because still no one talked. They just stared at us like we had both lost our minds.

So, I tried to explain how we wore our heavy-duty leather motorcycle gear, with our helmets, boots, leather gloves and our complete head gear for protection. I told them that we were really cautious and we had even taped our pant legs and our sleeves with duct tape so that the bees couldn't climb inside of our clothes. But that didn't seem to help either, because they all just looked at us like they were going to send us to a nursing home.

Darrell tried to help out by saying, "If it helps, the bees were actually killed by wasps. In fact they were already dead by the time Mr. Macy, the mayor, Mr. Riley, the two state policemen and your mom and I arrived. That's why most of them are cut in half."

Still no one talked. They just stood there and stared at us like we were talking in a foreign language.

After a few moments our son-in-law Ryan walked over and looked at the bees again and shook his head up and down and said with a huge smile across his face, "Well, they sure are...big!"

Our son-in-law Jeff, put his hand on Darrell's arm and calmly said, "No, where did you really get the bees?"

I finally just turned around and went in the house to get the ice cream and cones. I silently said to myself, "Telling the kids about the bees was a lot more difficult than I ever dreamed it would be. Good thing we don't have to tell them about the Lewiston Hill tunnel, Dr. Samuel Rodgers and all of the research documents or the key weather center of the world that is inside of the mountain. I don't think they would understand."

As I walked outside I pleasantly changed the subject and said "Who wants an ice cream cone?"

As everyone ate ice cream cones, they started talking again, but no one talked about the bees except for our three youngest grandchildren, Greyson, Kennedy and Emerson. The three of them were all sitting on a blanket out on the lawn eating their ice cream cones and I heard Greyson lean over and whisper to Kennedy, "Can you believe that our Grandpa and Grandma are real spies and they went to Grangeville and saved the world from all of those giant bees?"

Kennedy whispered back, "Well, I'm not sure if they are really spies, they are more like superheroes."

Our littlest cherub Emerson just nodded her head up and down and licked the ice cream off of her face; she was too busy eating her ice cream cone to do anything else. All of a sudden she flipped her hand out to make some profound comment, and as she bent over towards her sister, she dropped the whole top of her ice cream down Kennedy's leg. Kennedy instantly leaped up, and started jumping around and squealing.

As Kennedy danced around dripping in ice cream, Greyson just sat quietly on the blanket and nonchalantly repeated, "No...They're Spies."

All of the family went home around 11:00 p.m. Later that night as we were getting ready to go to bed, in our own bed, in our own house, I had to chuckle because how many Grandmas get to be known as a superhero spy?

As I sat down to pray, I thought, "Wow, What a week...hmm...what a month...hmm...what a year...hmm...what a life."

Dr. Rodgers was right; there is nothing more important in this world than your family.

I had recently completed a bible study presented by Beth Moore. Her acknowledgment sums it up best.

NOT ALL HAVE FAITH...
BUT THE LORD IS FAITHFUL